Sleep-walker's Moon

Sleep-walker's Moon

by

Ella Thorp Ellis

Atheneum 1980 New York

For Catherine & Rudy

LIBRARY OF CONGRESS CATALOGING IN PUBLICATION DATA

Ellis, Ella Thorp.
Sleepwalker's moon.

SUMMARY: Though Anna is sent to stay with a family
she has always loved when her father
joins the army in 1942, she comes to realize, bitterly,
that she really does not belong among them.
[1. Identity—Fiction] I. Title.
PZ7.E4714Sl   [Fic]   79-22665
ISBN 0-689-30739-X

Published simultaneously in Canada by
McClelland & Stewart, Ltd.
Manufactured by R. R. Donnelley & Sons,
Crawfordsville, Indiana
Designed by M. M. Ahern
First Edition

Sleep-walker's Moon

1

It was one of those still summer mornings peculiar to California beach towns, when even the roosters stop crowing and the grasshoppers pause and all you hear is the sound of the surf, as regular and soft as the echo of a heartbeat. On this particular morning there was also the rattle of my father's old car, carrying him off to war, but I was furious with him and chose not to listen.

Still, I couldn't *see* the ocean a mile away, and from where I stood alone in the alley, our old Ford's cloud of dust tunneling toward the highway, like a ball of loco weed, bouncing along, was the only moving thing *to* watch. So I stared until he turned off and the last of his dust settled back to earth, leaving nothing but bare sky where the alley dead-ended into the highway.

Then I opened the gate and turned into the garden. I was not ready to go back into the kitchen yet, where my new family sat around the table waiting for me. And even my father had loved this garden, though yesterday he had been disappointed when his favorite Santa Rosa plums weren't ripe. His last chance for a good plum until after the war, he'd said, with his embarrassed little laugh, a laugh that always sounded creaking, as if it hadn't been used in years and needed oiling. Maybe he was as shy as I was and I'd inherited that from him too. If so, it was another black mark against him, as far as I was concerned.

But I felt drawn to the old plum tree, so old that each year everyone was grateful when it actually blossomed and gave fruit, and I walked over and put my arms around its rough, cracked bark and leaned my face on its trunk, smelling a sweetness that came from the bark as well as the ripening fruit.

I knew its rough bark well, for every June I ran out to make sure the plum had set fruit when I returned to spend the summer with the Raymond family, much as another person might check on an elderly relative. But my father wouldn't be coming back for me this year because I was to live with Dr. Raymond for the "duration." This was the summer of 1942, and the United States had been at war for six months.

I was fourteen and I had wanted to be a Raymond for the last seven years. Once I had even tried to change my name from Anna to Raymona, but their daughter, Paula, said I lacked character and wouldn't speak to me until I changed back.

So it wasn't that I was mad at my father for going off to war, though I understood his patriotism no more than I understood anything else about this gentle, silent man with whom I'd spent my life. It seemed to me that we'd lived alone forever in musty three-room apartments in middle-sized cities, reading and eating pork chops. No, it wasn't his going off to war. In fact, when he'd hesitated, worried about leaving me alone, I'd told him to go ahead, practically pushing him out the door, desperate that I might lose the chance to come here. The strangest, hurt look had come over his face, and I had thought he understood then, and I felt terrible. Guilty. Not that I wished him any harm, for at fourteen I thought wars meant heroes rather than death.

I only wanted to live with the Raymonds. I might not have felt this way if he hadn't left me here every summer to get used to having a family. But he did, and I found a ready-made family. The Raymonds had a beautiful mother, a powerful father, a blonde princess sister, and an unpredictable little brother. Or so I thought when I was seven, the year I decided to become their second daughter. Still, I'd always assumed my father would be there too, that he wanted to be with all of us, sitting around the kitchen table together. Until last night.

I should have known. He'd hinted as much before we left. He'd looked around the pea green gloom of our windowless kitchen and said, "We've had a good time here, Anna, so you've that to remember." Totally satisfied! I was so surprised, I couldn't say a word. Besides, what can you say when your father's going off to war?

Then, last night at dinner, I'd looked up when we were all laughing, and he'd been poker-faced. He always played with his fork when he was bored, and he'd been twirling that fork all through dinner. If it had been one of us, Rosamund would have reached over and tapped us on the hand. At first I thought perhaps he missed his meat, since the Raymonds were vegetarians, but I saw him looking over at his book lying on a table in the living room and I knew. He wanted to pick up that book and start reading, right there at the table, on his last night with us. Of course, my father is an historian, an intellectual, but Hans is a doctor and Rosamund was an English teacher before she married Hans and had Paula, and they don't read at the table.

The truth was that my father was a man who thought three human beings together constituted a crowd and the only excuse for more than three, any three, was an earthquake or a flood. And it had apparently never occurred to him that I might feel differently. *That's* what I couldn't forgive. He was either blind or he didn't care. He'd even been surprised when I'd wanted to come here, suggesting I might prefer living with his brother (who was a sculptor) in Washington, D.C. I'd been coming here for seven summers, and he didn't even know I had to come to the Raymonds. He didn't even know it was natural. And I'd thought he understood, and I'd felt so terrible. That's what hurt, what made me feel like a fool.

Well, so what? Was I going to spend all morning hugging a plum tree? Hans was probably looking out the kitchen window thinking I was miserable about my father going off to war and asking his wife, Rosamund, if he should come and pry me loose from the tree, and Rosamund was probably saying it would be better to let me work it out for myself. Even though he was a country doctor and saw all kinds, he'd never understand my being mad at my father when he was going away to war. Never. For that matter, Hans liked people so well that he would never understand my father choosing to eat dinner with the newspaper, either.

That thought cheered me enough so that I gave the plum tree a final pat and started up the sidewalk toward the kitchen, prepared to suffer sympathy. From the outside, the Raymond house looked something like a wooden circus tent. Not the round kind but one of those oblong tents with a high pitched top. Hans had his medical office, waiting room, and bedrooms on one side of the house and the kitchen and living areas on the other, separated enough so that his daughter, Paula, and I had to hide in the closet in order to hear what was going on in the office.

Hans had built the house himself, and he'd built the kitchen so that it was only separated from the living room by shoulder high bookcases, so that Rosamund wouldn't be left out of any conversation when she was working there. This kitchen was the heart of the house and the kitchen table was where we gathered, where I knew the family was waiting for me. Hans had built the table three years before from an oak slab that a patient had given him, raising the floor under it so the table was high enough for Rosamund to work at comfortably but low enough for Paula and me to touch the floor with our feet.

Then Hans had bolted the table to the floor and built in benches so more people could fit around it. I must have been eleven and Paula twelve that summer, and we were both proud as peacocks to have a table made to our measure. So we didn't mind sitting hour after hour dangling our legs while Hans made sure we'd be comfortable at his new table. The measurement had to allow for our growth, too, and all the grown-ups had their own ideas about how tall Paula and I would turn out to be, though everyone allowed that I'd be the heavier if I didn't lay off the cheese sandwiches. Roger was only seven and hadn't gotten his growth yet, but he said he didn't mind resting his feet on a box until he did.

Thinking about the table made it easier to smile as I opened the door and slid in next to Rosamund at one end. Hans sat across from us, and Paula and her brother, Roger, were along the back side. They were drinking cocoa and looked up at me as if they were expecting something more than they saw. A small bowl of my favorite red roses stood in the center of the table. Rosamund must have picked them especially. It was the kind of thing she did. Rosamund was a stickler for other people's right to privacy, and sometimes you had to notice your roses on the table to realize she had been thinking about you.

"How about some cocoa, Anna?" she asked.

"Oh, yes, please."

"We get marshamallows because of your dad going away, too." Roger added. Roger was still young enough that marshmallows could make his day, and we seldom got them since Hans thought sugar was a poison.

"He get off OK?" Hans asked gently.

"You ought to know, Daddy. You were glued to the window watching," Paula said, and we all laughed. It was so like Hans.

The cocoa was Han's specialty, and I watched as he fussed over mine, adding butter and cinnamon and cream and whipping it up with an egg beater. My father used to say Hans looked like a baby buffalo, and he certainly charged around that small kitchen. He was a barrel-chested, hairy man, short and heavy boned, and he tended to walk slightly hunched over, which may have come from bending over patients on the treatment table.

"Well, Annie, you think you're going to be able to put up with us?" he asked, with that happy questioning look of a four year old. I loved that look.

"Sure thing."

"Sure you're not bored yet?"

"Daddy! She hasn't even been here twenty-four hours. How can she be bored?" Paula asked.

"Give her time," Roger said.

I shook my head, drinking it all in—cocoa, roses, everyone sitting around the table again, being here.

Rosamund spoke then, slowly, as she did when thinking something through by hearing her own words aloud.

"Paula," she said, looking up to make sure she had

her daughter's attention. They looked so much alike that I wondered if Paula ever thought, that's me in twenty years. The main difference was something I'd only noticed the night before. Paula's face had clouded up in the last year and looked tight next to the pleasure in her mother's face. But anyone would look like a dried-up fig next to Rosamund. Something in her expression made you feel hopeful, or perhaps peaceful, just looking at her, and that was probably why everyone said the doctor's missus was the most beautiful woman ever to hit South County. What set her apart from other pretty women, I decided, was that her beauty made the other person feel better, too. Still, she and Paula looked enough alike to send shivers down my spine, especially seeing them measuring each other out of those blue-grey eyes. Wide set, steady eyes. They wouldn't be easy women to lie to. And, at this moment, Paula knew her mother wanted something.

"Paula, when do you start work at the flower seed farms?" Rosamund asked.

"Monday. Delphiniums are early this year."

Rosamund pursed her lips. "They *are* early. Do you suppose there's any chance of getting Anna on, at least part of the summer?"

Paula pursed *her* lips. "Probably not. I'll try, Mother. I said I'll try, but I doubt it very much. Nothing personal, Anna, but my boyfriend's father owns this farm, and they only hire experienced flower seed pickers.

David had a hard enough time getting him to take me on, and I've worked in the garden here for years."

Hans and Roger looked at each other, and then Hans snorted.

"Well, I *have*, and it's slave labor, too. Mother, make them stop," Paula said.

"Hush, you two. Behave yourselves. I was thinking it would give Anna something to do, and she'll need money for clothes when she starts high school this fall."

Paula nodded and shrugged. She looked unhappy.

"Never mind. I don't need to work," I said quickly.

Hans winked at Roger and cleared his throat, a sign he had something to say. "Never mind, Mother, we can use Annie in the garden here at home. She couldn't be less use than Miss Paula and she might be more. Mr. Steffans can teach her to weed. Annie, I'll pay you the same as Roger gets, and you can learn a thing or two about the plant world. Would you like that?"

"If she can't get the hang of Mr. Steffan's lectures, I'll give her a hand. Unlike my sister, I know a weed from a rose," Roger said.

"A weed is merely an undiscovered flower," Paula retorted.

I looked at Roger gratefully. The old Greek next door, who talked religion to his plants and bayed at the full moon, had always frightened me. I'd managed to keep away from him, and I didn't want *his* help.

"You don't need to pay me. I don't want to go to

the beach by myself, so as long as Paula's working, I might as well learn to garden," I said, and tried to make my voice sound cheerful, though I couldn't help thinking about the other summers when Paula and I had spent our days at the beach and our nights listening to the big bands on the radio. Paula played the piano and the violin. We'd lie there in the dark, and she'd tell me to listen for the trombone's wail and then a few minutes later for some other instrument, and pretty soon I could begin to hear the separate sounds, too, and put them together the way the members of the band were doing, so I'd know when something beautiful was coming and look out for it. I'm pretty atonal, and so it had taken Paula three summers to teach me, but she kept at it, and I can hear music now, though I have to stop and listen.

But something strange was happening this year. The night before Paula had disappeared into the office as soon as dinner was over and stayed on the phone with her boyfriend until Hans exploded about her tying up the phone, which was important since he was the only doctor in town. Then she slammed downstairs to her room to put up her hair, something she'd never done before, which took the better part of an hour, and which Roger called her medieval torture rite. I kept waiting for her to come upstairs again. Other years, when I shared her room, I would have sat on her bed and talked, regardless of what she was doing. But last night I just waited with the grown-ups. Then she had another phone call and went to bed and turned off the light. I had my own cottage out in the garden now that I'd be living here, so there was no chance to talk as we went to sleep.

She wasn't unfriendly, but she hadn't been marking off the days on her calendar until I came the way she used to. That was for sure. Maybe she didn't *really* know I'd arrived, I thought, looking across the table and catching her eye. Paula smiled at me then and I knew. That was the way she smiled at Roger, who was twelve, when she thought he was a good kid. I was getting her good-kid smile! She thought I was a kid just because she'd finished a year of high school. And had a boyfriend. And a job. And there was something else—the lipstick, the pompadour, the way she walked—I sat there looking at Paula, surreptitiously now, conscious of my bitten nails. But she was only a *year* older. We'd been like sisters. Well, wasn't Roger her brother?

So I sat there like a balloon losing air, with two holes where my father and Paula used to be. And I was seeing our old Ford bumping down the alley. I was alone. It was not very reasonable to feel alone when you were sitting at a table with four other people, drinking cocoa, so I shivered and tried to pull myself together. Hans and Roger were still talking about using me in the garden, but I couldn't concentrate on what they were saying because of this new feeling of being absolutely alone, a feeling I couldn't remember ever having had before. Then I saw that Hans was watching me. Everyone had stopped talking.

I cleared my throat the way Hans did, and they laughed. "If it's OK, I think I'd like to walk on down and take a look at the beach," I said and looked over at Paula, unable to ask her to come but hoping she might.

"Go on ahead, poor baby, you've had a hard time," Hans said, putting an arm around me.

"I'd come with you but I've got to wash my hair," Paula said, and I told myself she did sound as if she wished she could come.

I slipped out from under Hans's arm. I wanted to tell him he didn't know what he was talking about, but I just shook my head.

"Be back in time for lunch, Anna. I'll make a salad," Rosamund called as I went out the door.

I started down the one paved street in town (aside from the highway, of course), passing gardens planted in brokendown car chassis, squash plants and gladiolas, whose snakelike spikes were only starting to show color and still looked ready to strike. I hated gladiolas. Climbing roses ran rampant over the houses and perfumed the air. And what I heard was still the roll and retreat of the surf, as regular as the echo of a heartbeat.

I think I had some vague idea of making contact with my town again, of marking my territory. Hans was the doctor, and I was the girl who lived at the Doc's. I was on first-name terms with most of the five hundred people in town, and nothing normally gave me more pleasure than catching up on the news. It was an ordinary enough packing shed town, I suppose. Hans said it provided a railroad for surrounding truck farms, and groceries and bars and housing for the workers; the men and women from Oklahoma and Mexico and the Philippines who had come with the Depression to start a new life. Hans always said he'd come with Rosamund and baby Paula about the same time and hung out his shingle and started trying to keep the workers alive.

Normally, I would have stopped and chatted three times in as many blocks, but this new feeling of aloneness was still on me and, as I got used to it, a soothing melancholy settled in, and I merely waved to people in their yards; waved and walked on, not thinking anymore. Perhaps hoping the town and the sea could sink in and cure me of my loneliness before I went home to lunch.

2

WORKING IN THE GARDEN with Hans and Roger those first days gave me time to settle in. Weeding under the honeysuckle, I could absorb the newly curled and dating Paula. After all, I was living with the Raymonds and I wouldn't be leaving in September. I'd be going to high school with Paula, I thought, as I hoed around the roses. I wouldn't seem so much younger when we were running for the bus together, walking in the halls together. I could wait. I knew how to wait.

Meanwhile, I was safe. I could finally be like everyone else. Anonymous. Living alone with my father had always made me a sitting duck for people who liked to be sorry for someone, and this last year had been a particular disaster. First, I'd started my period and nearly went mad trying to find out *what to do about that* without asking any questions. Library indexes aren't all they're cracked up to be if you're not given to asking. And ads leave out everything but the sunset. I thought I'd figured it out, though, and was about to tackle buying a brassiere when our homeroom teacher kept all the girls after school one day last April for a heart-to-heart talk. After that talk, I wanted to die. But I couldn't even get my father to let me quit school. He kept asking why, and, of course, I couldn't say a word. All I could do was wait for the three–ten dismissal bell and run the twelve blocks home.

That was all over, though, I thought as I walked along behind Hans while he showed Roger and me the weeding he wanted done. I had another chance. I would never have to think about that again.

"Well, how do you like my Garden of Eden, Annie?" Hans asked, and his smile was vulnerable. He loved every flower.

Like it? I was Eve, and God didn't have to worry about me eating any apples. I'd choose His garden any day. "It's a fairyland," I said.

"I think so, too, baby," Hans said, smiling. "Well, I've got to get back to the patients. You and Roger carry on."

I watched him walk slowly out to the front garden. He opened the gate on a woodsy park with benches set about under redwoods and pines, where patients could relax while they waited for the doctor. Hans said the good karma coming from the trees helped people get well. He stopped to help an old man to his feet, and arm in arm they walked through the front door to his office.

I was glad he'd left me alone with Roger, glad that old Mr. Steffans was off working. Roger was peaceful. Actually Roger reminded me somewhat of my father, quiet and drawn apart, but friendly. I knew how to take him. Everyone else in the family seemed to love him best, but I'd noticed they were a little afraid of him, too. Not that he threw his weight around. He never did that. But he usually got his way.

For example, ever since I first met the Raymonds, they'd eaten mashed potatoes three or four times a week. The only starch Roger liked turned out to be mashed potatoes. I never heard him complain, nor ask his mother to fix them, but it would have been hard for Rosamund to see him leave the table hungry. There isn't too much to eat in a vegetarian household besides starches and vegetables. They were a treat for me because my father wasn't about to peel and boil and mash potatoes after coming home from a day's work. Mashed potatoes were one of those things that only come with a live-in mother. Still, I sometimes wondered if Paula didn't get tired of mashed potatoes, year after year.

As long as I'd known him, Roger had a box of treasures hidden under his bed. He would sit cross-legged on his bed, going over his treasures for hours. He liked nothing better than taking them out and holding each piece of potentially precious quartz rock, or gold eyeglasses, or sea-colored float up to the light. And when he said the green float must have bobbed across the ocean from Japan, I could see his brown eyes following that bobbing glass ball over all the thousands of miles of sea. He also collected coins and, by showing his collection to visitors, had added to it considerably since I'd seen it the summer before.

His collecting had made him much more organized as a gardener than his father. So Roger and I weeded rose beds that first day, the geranium and vegetable garden the next day, and started on the orchard by the third day. In this way we had covered most of the back yard, and I had been with the Raymonds over a week when Paula came home one day and announced that she'd gotten me a job in the flower seed fields, picking with her.

We were at dinner, the scene of most of our confrontations, and I had a feeling that Paula was daring somebody, though I didn't know who or why.

I did know that I didn't want to work at the seed

farms, or anywhere else outside the Raymond garden. Hans had the ability to share responsibility, and I felt those plants already depended on me. For Hans, each rose was a patient in precarious health, and I woke every morning to the perfume of two hundred blooming rose bushes, and I could hardly wait to get out among them, as worried as any ward nurse. Hans said I had the hands of a gardener and the memory of a librarian. Rosamund said it was always such a relief when Hans found someone else to talk gardening with so she could get on with her own work.

On the other hand, how could I let Paula down after she'd gone out of her way to get me this job, marching right up to her boyfriend's father and *asking* him to take me on? I would never have had such courage.

"But I have to help in the garden," I whispered, looking around the table for support.

No one said anything. Everyone seemed to be looking down, except Paula, who was staring at me, so I finally let my eyes rest on an orange bowl filled with loganberries that Roger and I had picked only an hour before. We'd had the berries with whipped cream for dinner. Not as dessert, but an entire dinner of loganberries and cream.

"See, Mother, what did I tell you? I get her a job paying twice what she makes here, and *she* wants to muck around in the garden." Paula's face strained again, and her voice shook.

"Anna just feels a responsibility for our garden, that's all. Of course, she'll take the field job. She'll need the money for clothes when you girls go back to school, and the back yard is almost weeded, anyhow."

Hans was going to teach me to prune, I wanted to shout, but how could I argue with Rosamund? I looked over to Hans for help, but he was nodding and drawing lines on his napkin with his fork, quick, impatient lines.

"At least you know a hoe from a rake now," he said, avoiding my eyes.

So it was settled. All he remembered was that he'd had to show me how to tell a hoe from a rake. He'd also said that I had the hands of a gardener. I kept waiting for him to say something further.

We sat there at the table. The silence sucked at my nerves like a vacuum. Rosamund and Roger looked as if they'd left for another planet and only their bodies sat dutifully on at the table. Their hands lay folded on their laps. We'd all stopped eating. Paula and Hans glared at each other, their hands clutching the edge of the table in the same gesture. Was I to blame? I felt sick to my stomach. But I *was* taking the job, and Hans didn't care, so what was this impending earthquake all about, anyway? Using my father's term for a family squabble cheered me enough so I could break the silence, though my voice shook.

"Thanks for the job, Paula. That's great of you. I

was just worried about leaving the garden unweeded but—"

"But to Paula that's just mucking around," Hans burst out. "She's too much of the money-hungry young lady—our little gardening expert—to dirty her hands at home these days. Or maybe it's the boyfriend? Once those hormones get going, she can't muck around her home anymore, no siree!" Hans brought his fist down on the table, rattling dishes.

I stared. I'd never seen anyone bang his fist on a table.

Paula merely shrugged, keeping her face down, stirring her berries and cream round and round into a lavender paste. Then, suddenly, she did look up, catching her father's eye.

"You always said you were giving us experience in our garden so we could get a good job. All right, I've got one."

"That's a *good* job?" Hans sputtered, but he looked embarrassed.

"Pays three times what you pay us," Paula said.

Hans turned to Rosamund, then. "Mucking around, she called it, Mother. Mucking around in our *garden!*"

I took a deep breath. So I wasn't to blame. This was between Paula and Hans. I'd seen them fight before, but never like *this!* What was eating Hans?

"Oh, that's just an expression kids use these days." Rosamund laughed quietly, taking up her fork again.

"I remember saying twenty-three-skiddoo to my mother and she didn't like it, either. Would anyone like some more berries?" she asked, as if there had never been a break in the conversation. Sometimes I thought Rosamund really did take her mind somewhere else when there was trouble in the family.

"Oh, yes, please. This is my best and favorite dinner," Roger said, smiling at his father. Hans looked fiercer than ever, and his right hand gripped his fork as if he might use it violently, but Roger just kept on smiling.

Then Roger and his mother began talking about the loganberries Hans was growing this year versus the inferior blackberries they used to get from patients. Paula still looked down into the berries she was stirring, and her father still clenched his fork, but Roger and Rosamund, ignoring them, discussed berry size, sweetness, even fertilizers. I knew that few subjects interested Rosamund less than fertilizers so I was fascinated. It was like watching a performance, maybe a tennis game. I knew they were conspirators, even before I saw Roger wink at his mother.

Hans must have seen the wink, too, for his hand relaxed and his face cleared and a moment later he laughed. "All right, Mother, but I wish I'd been there to see the look on your mother's face when you told *that* one to skiddoo."

So it was over, a fury that spent itself in a few minutes, leaving only Paula sullen and silent. Roger and his mother had brought peace back to the table. I was annoyed at Paula's silence, forgetting that all she'd done was go out of her way to get me a job as her mother had asked her to do. I counted on Paula's honesty. But I wanted her to pretend there'd been no fight:

Because the fight left me shaken, I went to my room right after dinner and lay in the dark. My father didn't fight, and I'd never seen such an explosion at the Raymond's before, either. Hans and Paula had always rubbed each other's nerves and this wasn't any different, I told myself, but I knew this fury was worse, and as I lay there in the dark, in my room, hearing through the open windows the cheerful bustle of Roger and Paula doing the dishes, I began to feel lonely. Someone put on a polka record, and the gaiety sounded forced and false, like a radio soap commercial. Far off, I heard the cry of a single owl, and it echoed and called again and I listened to that owl for a long time. I could not be sure that no other owl answered, but every call had the same tentative questioning tone as if the bird were uncertain to whom he called. Like me.

However, the next morning I was up and dressed when Paula knocked on my door at six. We were to start work at seven and had at least a half-hour walk to the flower fields.

"I'd forgotten you were one of those morning people," Paula said. "I'm still half-asleep."

"My father and I always went for a walk at six and so I wake up automatically. Can't help it," I shrugged.

"How come? A walk with your father?" Paula sounded amazed.

"I don't know. Ever since I can remember we went for a walk. I guess he liked to be out before the street-cars so he could hear the birds. He's crazy about birds, like your mother." I shrugged again because Paula was still watching me.

"I can't *imagine* walking with Daddy every morning. Did you like it?"

"It was just something we did, like eating and sleeping. Yes, I guess I really loved it because I'm looking forward to walking to work. Aren't you?"

"Hardly, but maybe it will be better now that you're here," Paula replied, and we fell silent as we started out, each thinking our own thoughts.

I was excited. This was the first time I would be hired, paid by someone who didn't know me, and I felt as if I were setting out on a pilgrimage. The sun was just rising, flooding the sky with soft beginnings of color. Wisps of fog swept along beside us, making our alley mysterious and strangely new. Only the roosters are awake, I thought. Paula and I smiled at each other.

But as we passed the old Greek's house next door, I heard a squeaking pump and a great splashing of water, and then a muttering and snorting, which might have been either swearing or praying. Through his fruit trees I could see Mr. Steffans, a solid bull of a man, barefoot and naked to the waist. Fog curled about him and he did look like old Merlin, the wizard. He rubbed himself briskly with a towel, this man who'd been too sick to help in the garden, and then started a chant that sent shivers up my spine and woke every dog within a block. It had an eerie, reedlike sound, rather like that of a tuning fork, and I looked at Paula, but she only shrugged. Maybe she heard this every morning, but I'll bet the neighbors thought he was the strangest man in town. I wanted to ask, but I hesitated to say his name aloud, to attract his attention, so I hurried silently after Paula.

At the next corner we turned toward the highway, walking under eucalyptus trees we'd climbed when we were younger, which now peppered us with seed balls and dew. Coming out onto the strawberry beds that ran alongside the highway meant coming into the first morning sunshine, and it felt warm and good. The creek where we had learned to swim burbled along beside us. All we had to do was follow the footpath to the edge of the mesa road and we'd reach the seed farms.

So I was surprised when Paula abruptly crossed the highway, urgently motioning me to follow her.

"He stares at me," Paula whispered, pointing out a dilapidated old Victorian house, set well back from the highway in a tangled mass of bushes. All the shades in the house were drawn, and it didn't look to me as if anyone had lived there in a hundred years.

"Who?"

"The dirty old man who lives there," Paula said, going on to explain that she crossed the street because, though she'd never yet seen him in the morning, sometimes when she was coming home alone he would stand in the driveway with his finger crooked, beckoning her to come with him. Then she would run as fast as she could to the corner. There, sometimes, she'd stop and look back and he'd still be standing, beckoning.

"He must be crazy," I said, shivering. Actually, that beckoning was what I found so frightening about Mr. Steffans, our next-door neighbor. He had been forever beckoning the last summer I visited the Raymonds. It always turned out he only wanted me to see the first pomegranate on his tree or something like that, but it *was* scary. I didn't blame Paula, and I suspected she'd gotten me the job for company. After last night's fight, I decided not to ask, but I liked to think she needed me.

"Either crazy or over-sexed," Paula said matter-of-factly. "He's filthy and old and spits tobacco. Just the sort you'd want to kiss you. Let alone—"

"Let alone what?" I asked, still thinking of Mr. Steffans.

"Do you know the facts of life?" Paula asked as we drew across from the house.

Trust Paula to come right out and ask. But, as for the facts of life, I knew that babies came out of a mother's stomach and the father got them there, but I was somewhat hazy on the process.

"Never mind," Paula said. "Sometime when Daddy's gone, I'll show you in his medical books. There's even one on chastity belts."

"Wow. Great," I said, though I hadn't any idea what chastity belts were.

"Shhhhh—we're going by now." Paula had clutched my arm, and we tiptoed by the haunted house across the highway, casing each window to see where the old man was leering out at us.

A dog howled, and I screamed.

"What? Where?" Paula hissed, letting go my arm and starting to run.

I ran too, trying to decide whether to admit I hadn't seen anything but the dogs.

"I'm not sure. Maybe I could have seen a shade move," I lied breathlessly when we slowed down.

"See, I knew it! I know he's staring when I go by."

"Just like Mr. Steffans," I whispered.

"Oh—him!" Paula's tone left no doubt that old Merlin was simply not in the same league with her dirty old man. But he wasn't always wagging his finger at her the way he did at me.

"At least there are two of us, and we can stick together," I said hopefully.

Paula looked at me doubtfully, but she nodded her head and that was enough for me.

"We'll be like sisters," I whispered, but not loudly enough for Paula to hear. I'd tried that before, and she'd said I was a *friend*. But I had always wanted a sister so much that my father finally told me to stop trying to marry him off.

I was so absorbed that I didn't realize we had arrived until Paula turned up a dirt road leading to an old farmhouse. I looked up then and found I was surrounded by fields and fields of giant blue delphiniums as tall as Paula and I. Everywhere I turned, there were stalks of delphiniums in blocks of colors ranging from palest blue to deep purple. Sky colors. It looked as though someone had made a giant quilt of blues, a quilt stretching clear from the mesa to town. And when I looked up at the sky, it seemed washed out by comparison.

"Isn't this the most beautiful—" but I stopped in mid-sentence when I saw that Paula was watching a tall blond boy who was running toward us. I had never seen him before, but I was sure that this must be David, her boyfriend.

3

AT FIRST I was disappointed in David. He was a tall, gawky boy whose yellow hair fell over his face like straw and who moved as if he were continually surprised at the length of his arms and legs and couldn't think where to set them down. He reminded me of one of those elasticized puppets with beaded arms and legs that fall all in a heap when you press hard on their springboard. Even his head and shoulders moved with the jerk of his arms and legs. Paula said he played football and basketball, but it was pretty hard to visualize him doing anything but fumbling.

However, though I was disappointed in David's looks, I liked him right away. He had a gentle smile; it lit his face, so that, like the Cheshire cat, his smile seemed to stand alone. Also, he treated Paula as if she were the queen of England, so possibly he knew he was no great match for a girl as beautiful as Paula. When she told David about the old man who scared her, he offered to walk to the Raymond house every morning and then walk us back to work.

"My daddy would come after you with his BB gun," Paula said.

"Your daddy is the only man in the valley without a twenty-two. The Elks are thinking of taking up a collection for him." David laughed.

"Better not. He uses that BB gun, don't you forget."

David laughed again, but he'd heard the tales of Doc spraying BB's at intruders, and I knew he wouldn't be walking us to work against Paula's father's wishes. I was glad because I didn't want to share Paula every morning.

They were smiling at each other, so I turned and looked back at the delphinium fields and the sun rising beyond. A faint breeze stirred the flowers so they seemed to surge toward me, and suddenly I wanted to run through the field, zigzagging the rows, rolling in flowers, rolling until I dropped from exhaustion. Then I would sleep and wake up fresh, surrounded by delphiniums. I must have said so aloud because David answered me.

"You won't think they're so great by the end of the day when your fingers rub raw," he grumbled. Still, he blushed, and I thought he was pleased. These were his father's fields, after all.

"Didn't you bring us gloves?" Paula frowned.

David nodded, but he looked unhappy. He scuffed the sand at the end of the rows. "I brought rubber gloves this time. They probably won't do as much, but maybe you can pick faster. My father—"

Paula reached out and took David's hand and smiled up at him. "I know," she said. "No one else uses gloves, and it makes him nervous. Makes us different."

"Slower," David amended gently, taking Paula's free hand, so the two of them stood there, holding both hands and smiling at each other. I'd never seen Paula look so beautiful.

"Why don't the other workers wear gloves? They cost too much?" I asked.

"Thirty-nine cents. No, they slow you down," David explained gently. "Hands toughen up in a day or two, Anna."

"They do not. Wear those gloves or they'll tear your hands to pieces."

"My hands are a mess, anyway. I don't need gloves," I said.

David shrugged, and we both stood looking at Paula.

"You could try it without gloves, for starters." David sighed.

"Anna, it's not fair for you to go home with hands all cut up so Daddy has to worry about you, too. Think of somebody else, for a change. After all, you're paid by the hour."

"OK." I said it casually so it didn't sound like a promise, for I intended to pick without gloves. Nobody else looked like a basket case. Paula didn't own me, and she didn't have a corner on the world's good sense, either. If my hands got bad, then I'd put on the gloves.

The three of us stood silently for a moment, and then Paula sighed. "I'm not trying to tell you how to run your life, Anna. It's just that Daddy thinks every cut means gangrene will set in. OK? I got you this job, and so he'll blame *me* if anything happens to you. Understand?"

"Yes. Don't worry, Paula. I do see your point," I said, weighing the words.

Then David gave Paula a quick hug before setting out to get the gunny sacks we wore around our waists during the picking. Paula showed me how to snap off each flowerlet separately, dropping it into the sack before going on to the next, working up the stalk. We were only to pick those pods that had already gone to seed.

"What happens if I pick the wrong ones, Paula?"

"Most of them will dry out anyway so don't worry. Dave's father just wants them picked before a big wind comes up and blows them into the next county." Paula, happy again, hummed as she picked two particularly big delphiniums and wove them through the band of David's hat. Then she picked smaller flowers and decorated our hats, holding each up for inspection and then putting the finishing touches on the hats.

"I've never seen anything so beautiful," I said, though what I really meant was that I loved Paula for thinking of weaving flowers through our hats.

"Will you please stop using that word—beautiful— for one whole hour?" Paula asked, amused.

When David came back, he liked the hats too. We could see the other hands starting work, about half high school summer help like ourselves and the other half steady farmhands.

We each took a row, David working along with me until I got the hang of picking, which was simple enough if you played an eenie, meanie, minie, moe game of which flowerlets were ready to pick. Then he moved over to work next to Paula and, at first, their laughter made me feel left out, but then I thought that if I were still in San Francisco I'd have no place I wanted to be except the library. I saw myself spending the day alone in our pea green apartment, and I was glad to be out-side among delphiniums. Earning money.

And soon Paula started to sing. I knew most of the songs from the *Hit Parade*, and she and David taught me the ones I didn't know. The morning passed quickly, and it wasn't until we broke for lunch at eleven that I realized my arms were so sore I could hardly move them. In fact, every muscle in my body ached. My hands ached too, but the picking went much faster without the gloves, and my hands were cooler.

David and Paula walked hand in hand down to a willow-lined creek away from the other pickers. I'd hoped we might all be eating with the other pickers, but Paula and David wanted a little more privacy.

However, they didn't mind my being around, and after I got used to their kissing—which I had never done publicly myself—I rather liked being by ourselves, too. Paula, I discovered, was working just so they could be together (the money being secondary to her), although she thought what her father paid at home was slave wages and would never have considered that as a summer job. She did, however, hope to make real money as an accompanist in the fall. In fact, if her mother wouldn't let her go without me, I might even be able to come along.

I clapped my hands, surprised by their crackling report in the dappled stillness of the willows.

"You can't dance if you're accompanying," David grumbled.

"Then why don't you play your sax and we could do a duo and make some real money?" Paula asked.

"Oh, that's your game, is it?" David said softly. He didn't sound impressed.

Paula lay with her head in his lap and she stopped eating her sandwich and smiled up at him. "I mean it, you know. I want to play, and I want to earn some money with the piano."

"Fair enough," David said. "But don't start managing me just yet, little lady. Your mother said to take Anna, remember?"

Much as I wanted to go, there was something in David's tone that made me uncomfortable. I don't suppose any of us could have known how serious Paula was nor how stubborn David would turn out to be. He was, after all, her first boyfriend, and that was their first summer together.

But David was already uneasy that day under the lightly moving willows, and Paula already had to console him.

I swam as they necked, lazily floating with the current, long hair fanning out behind me, sunlight flecking the water with a photo reflection from overhanging willow leaves. I floated and I watched them, thinking how wonderful it must be to be in love. For theirs was a gentle caress, with whispered confidences and much giggling, a joyous light kiss and certainly not the passionate and frustrating kiss I had known with my one boyfriend. To whom I had, just the day before, sent off a letter in which one whole page had been repeatings of the word *love*. However, I never expected to see him again.

                    love,
                          love,
                                love,
                                      love,
                                            love,
                                                  love,
                                            love,
                                      love,
                                love,
                          love,
                    love,

I had written, having in mind a formation of migrating ducks and myself flying left wing, neither of which were allusions he was apt to appreciate.

Too soon, we had to go back to work. The afternoon started endless and grew steadily longer. I felt beyond singing, almost beyond aching, certainly beyond any hope of wearing rubber gloves, and I hated the smell and the colors of delphiniums. Those raucous blues could blind a person. Finally, at three, the overseer struck the quitting gong; all around me I heard pickers sigh. I staggered to the end of the row, flexing my cramped hands so I would be able to untie my apron and dump the last batch of seeds into the wax-paper-lined boxes. I couldn't walk another step, let alone home. Maybe a swim would revive me.

"Hurry up, Anna! They kept us half an hour overtime and I'll be late for my piano lesson and Daddy will have to pay, anyhow, and you know what that means. Come *on*, Annie . . . *move*."

I stared at Paula. You go on ahead and tell them I'll be along, I thought. I don't have a lesson so I'll stay and swim. Sounded reasonable. Sensible. But even then, as I stood under the burning sun, scuffing dust (a nervous habit that always wore out my left shoe), I knew I wouldn't say a word, not because of the beckoning old man or her father's temper, but because I hadn't the guts. Paula would have told me where to go if it had been my piano lesson and her first day at work, and I respected her for that. But I'd never argued with my father or anyone else, and for the first time in my life I wondered why. Not because I was a nice kid. I was a hypocrite. Here I was, Annie Milktoast, gathering up my sweater and lunchbox when all I wanted to do was throw them in her face and dive in the creek.

"Oh, Lord, look at your hands. Didn't I tell you to keep on your gloves? Didn't I? Darn you," Paula muttered as I came up to her.

I looked from my hands to Paula and back to my hands. They *were* pretty cut up, bleeding as a matter of fact. But she could have noticed I'd stopped biting my nails, couldn't she? Or she could have said it was too bad my hands were bleeding.

"Don't you *hear* me? But he'd never blame you. He'll blame *me*. Wait and see."

I shrugged. I was too tired for Paula's traumas this afternoon.

"You are the most selfish person I've ever met in my life," Paula yelled. The other pickers were looking at us.

"You'll be late for your piano lesson," I said. I was sorry to notice that David looked mad, too. "I'll pay you for the gloves on Friday," I told him.

He smiled and shook his head. If he was mad, it didn't seem to be at me. Tired as I was, that seemed important.

Paula turned on her heel then, without another word, and headed for home, trotting.

David and I followed, eating her dust, as he said. Those were the only words either of us spoke until he left me a block from home.

"You did well," he said then, leaving me wondering what I'd done well.

That evening Hans did see my hands and gently covered them in salve and then took me out into the garden and showed me how to pick a delphinium flower so that only the tips of thumb and forefinger were involved. He dropped each flower gently in a paper bag and had picked the stalk bare in less than half the time Paula and I could manage.

"I didn't know you could do that," Paula said.

"Why didn't you show Annie how to pick?" Hans asked, impatiently.

"You never showed *me*. I *told* her to wear rubber gloves," Paula replied, indignant.

"Nonsense. They're too awkward," Hans said.

And, even as I dreaded another fight, I was proud that Hans had shown *me*. He must feel I had some talent in the garden or he wouldn't have bothered. I tried to feel badly that he had shown me and not Paula, but I couldn't. It served her right, I thought, for being so bossy. Still, I had to admit he had blamed her as she said he would. I waited for her to say something more, but she did not.

We all stood quietly in the gathering dusk, each thinking our own thoughts. It was a warm evening and the smell of roses hung over the garden. Wind chimes tinkled gently and fireflies drifted across the zinnia bed like sparklers.

4

As WE GOT USED to each other and to the rhythms of field work, Paula and I settled into a comfortable routine. We would meet in the kitchen by 6:15 every morning, each of us silently making one Tillamook cheese sandwich for breakfast and two for lunch. Sometimes Roger would pass through on his way next door to bird watch with Mr. Steffans. Roger would smile and wave as he went out the kitchen door, but he didn't speak, either. For he knew, and I had learned, that Paula needed time to wake up before she could tolerate conversation. There was something peaceful and mysterious about our silent cooperation, and part of it was having Rosamund's kitchen to ourselves.

Conversation usually began with wishing Mr. Steffans a good morning as we passed him while he was giving himself a brisk rubdown by his squeaky pump. If we were a little late, Mr. Steffans might already be talking to his plants. He told his plants of his gout pains and his theories on reincarnation, for Mr. Steffans, though a good Greek, was also a Buddhist. He also talked of his homeland on Crete and the mad-dog Nazis who were starving his family. If he wasn't talking to his Belle of Portugal rose, he was talking to a philosopher named Paracelsus, who had been dead four hundred years. However, as long as Paula was along, as long as he wasn't wagging his finger for me to come into his garden, I had to admit old Merlin wasn't as hopeless as I'd thought. For one thing, it was amazing how many farmers thought he was more reliable than the weather reports. For another, he was Hans's chess partner and he usually beat him. So he had to have brains.

Anyway, one morning in early July, just before my birthday, Paula and I were walking by his house, and there was Mr. Steffans, lying under his zapota tree, moaning.

"We're late," Paula said.

"But something's wrong with Mr. S." I was worried but afraid to stop and go up to him.

Paula did stop, and turning, considered Mr. Steffans closely for a few minutes. "Well, he does have gout and it hurts like the devil," she began making a nursely diagnosis. "But I don't think that's it. I think he's talking to the white owl."

I thought she was out of her mind but she motioned for me to be quiet and so I was. Paula seemed to have forgotten we were late, something she never forgot.

Soon we heard another low, soft moaning, this one coming from inside the dense tree above Mr. Steffans. When the moan from the tree ceased, he started his own moaning again. Then, whatever it was in the tree had its turn.

This went on for some time, and I was becoming impatient. However, Paula stood mesmerized, not moving a muscle. She turned such a fierce look on me as I shifted my feet that I almost stopped breathing.

Suddenly we heard a loud rustling in the dense foliage, then a squawk that sounded like a chicken, and a white owl at least two feet tall flew down out of the tree and hovered over Mr. Steffans, his wingspread enormous.

I opened my mouth to scream, but Paula gently laid a restraining hand on my arm. The bird's headlight yellow eyes were fierce, and I could see terrible talons. I thought the bird intended to attack, but he hesitated, undecided, as if surprised at himself.

Mr. Steffans continued cooing, gently, even softer now that the great bird was near, and I saw that one hand was outstretched. It was only then that I noticed something in the old man's hand. I think it was a dead mouse, perhaps one of the thousands of field mice that shared the vacant lots with lizards and horny toads.

The white owl had seen the mouse before I had and was deciding whether to take it. When he finally darted down, I was surprised at the care with which his predator beak extracted the mouse from Mr. Steffans's hand, hovering again before he flew back into the tree with his prize hanging from his beak.

Mr. Steffans sat up then, grinning and waving toward us, silent still, like the animal trainer at the end of a circus act.

We waved back and continued on our way, lost in what we had just been privileged to see.

"Sometimes," Paula said half a block later, "sometimes the owl will stay on his hand and they talk to each other."

"Owls aren't even white," I said, trying to capture the full extent of the miracle.

"White owls come from Alaska and they're very rare, you know," Paula replied, sounding so like Roger's bird talks that I laughed.

"They are rare!"

I said nothing but I thought about that man with his bare feet swollen by gout, who fed owls, who had taught Roger more than professors knew about how birds lived, gave Rosamund advice on cooking, played chess with Hans, and made friends with plants.

"I guess he's something like an uncle for all of you," I said finally, thinking of my own uncle who wrote letters asking what I thought of the war or summer vacations, unanswerable essay questions. "How long has he been talking to owls?"

"Well, the first time he showed Roger that owl was two years ago, and I first saw it a few months ago. He says he's lost his way and can't get home, just like Mr. Steffans can't go home to Crete. Mr. Steffans collects exiles," Paula said, hurrying me so we wouldn't be late to work.

So he collected exiles, did he? No wonder he was forever trying to get me to come over and talk. He was trying to add me to his collection. Well, they could just stay exiles all they wanted, that garlicky, barefoot old man and the white owl, but they could count me out. Enough was enough. I was going to settle down. This was going to be my home, with Rosamund's help.

Rosamund had been taking me in hand, and if making me a beauty was out of the question, she was certainly improving the package. First, she had taken me to a beauty parlor and had my hair cut, and then to Sears and bought me three brassieres. Then came lessons on applying lipstick, a nail care kit, basic clothing styles for big-shouldered girls, and ten lessons in how to care for your clothes.

To Rosamund and to Paula, none of this was important, but simply a sensible approach to looking well, so I wouldn't be self-conscious and could settle down to studying. The comfortable thing about Rosamund was that she never pried. She saw what needed to be done and did it.

She probably had no way of knowing I was the most self-conscious fourteen year old she had ever met. She simply walked in and bought three brassieres. How could she know that I'd been wandering around foundation departments for months trying to get the courage to choose a bra and buy it so the boys would stop whistling "The Jersey Bounce" whenever I came walking down the hall? I kept pulling those bras out of their drawer a dozen times a day to reassure myself that I finally had them. I kept snapping the strap over my shoulder.

She also gave me a briefing on menstrual periods and sanitary napkins. It took all of five minutes. Suppose I'd been living with her last April. Would the homeroom teacher have kept us after school? Or, suppose she had, would I have assumed she was talking about me?

What happened was that the teacher kept all the girls after class and told us that at puberty girls began to smell, especially at certain times of the month. The teacher said she realized that not all the girls in the class had mothers who could help them in these matters, for one reason or another. There were other motherless girls in the class, but I was sure she meant me. Later, a girl who had never liked me and vice versa, said the teacher must have meant me. That confirmed it and I lived in terror and reeked of Lifebuoy soap the rest of the semester.

By July I began to suspect that if I *were* to tell Rosamund about the talk, which I would rather die than do, she would probably laugh and say the teacher was simply giving a routine health lecture, one she gave every term. And didn't all the girls tease each other later, she might have asked? I didn't stick around to find out, so I wouldn't know. Even if I didn't hold this conversation with Rosamund, going over it in my mind defused the terror somewhat. Rosamund's logic was a useful survival tool, even Rosamund's logic according to me.

I don't suppose I shall ever know how much Rosamund's short beauty course helped and how much my own self-confidence changed my luck, but by August the boys started noticing me.

Me?

I couldn't believe it. No longer was I floating down the river pretending to be Dorothy Lamour while Paula and David necked during the noon hour. We had company. Lots of company.

We had finished picking delphinium seeds by that time and had also gotten in the sweet pea seeds before the late summer fog could rot their pods. For weeks we'd been stumbling about, half dizzy with their heavy perfume. By August we were picking nasturtiums and early marigolds. My back and legs ached all the time. I was too tired for boys and wished they could wait until after we'd quit and bought our new clothes. I wanted to feel ready. I wanted to be my new self.

And there was something else. Everything was working out for me at the same time my father was being shipped to England, and it made me feel as if I'd gotten him out of the way so I could fly.

Then he wrote how proud he was to be helping Britain and how delighted to be seeing his uncles and aunts. I wrote back that I was terribly proud of him. Actually, I was relieved, but we all talked a lot about pride that summer. Possibly because we heard the word so often on the evening news in those early days of the war, before many people had been killed. Our only word came from the evening news, the one time when everyone in the Raymond kitchen was quiet. Rosamund and Hans's faces were drawn and tense while we listened, but for Paula and me, in those days before we knew soldiers and sailors ourselves, the war was far away, an adventure of my father's. Enlistment was an enviable dream for David, something he looked forward to after graduation if the war lasted another year, which we doubted.

I don't think Paula and David were very happy about what David called the wolf pack either, since it cramped their style. However, as long as the boys came from high school they limited themselves to making fun of them. But when Big Boy, our married overseer, started hanging around and teaching me phrases in Tagalog, "love phrases," David said, and I made the mistake of telling

Paula that Big Boy gave me goose pimples and wanted to take me to the movies, Paula decided I needed sex education.

5

BUT SHE DIDN'T SAY anything to me until one Saturday afternoon two weeks later when Rosamund, Hans, and Roger had gone to San Luis. Paula and I had stayed home because we didn't want to spend money, preferring to save it for new school clothes in San Francisco.

"All right," Paula said, as soon as we heard the car skid out of the alley toward the highway. "We'll give them a few minutes, just to make sure they haven't forgotten anything, then we can probably count on three hours."

"A few more minutes and then what?" I asked, excited. Last time everyone else had gone to San Luis, we'd gone through her mother's jewelry and then through Roger's collection. I had felt a little guilty, especially since Roger was always generous about showing me his precious things, but we hadn't taken or disturbed anything, and we'd had a wonderful time trying on the jewelry. Besides, Rosamund had promised Paula her turquoise squash-blossom necklace for her twenty-first birthday, so it was only natural that she should want to see how it looked from time to time.

"Today you are going to learn what's what with

your body so guys like Big Boy can't put anything over on you," Paula announced, hands on her hips.

That frightened me a bit, since she kept looking at her wristwatch and tapping her foot.

"OK," she said finally. "Sometimes Daddy forgets something and has to come back, so I always wait at least ten minutes. Let's go."

"Where?" I asked.

Paula merely beckoned, and I got up from the kitchen table and followed her into the hall. Once in the hall, Paula stealthily opened the door to her father's medical office and, motioning me to hurry, silently closed the door behind us. Now I *was* frightened. I knew we'd be in serious trouble if we were caught here because Hans kept his office sterile.

"Don't touch anything," Paula said, as if reading my mind.

She went straight to an old walnut bookcase and opened its glass doors. I could tell she knew what she was looking for.

As for me, I felt as if I were in church, close to mysteries I had no right invading. Everything had its place. Cupboards filled with surgical instruments, towels, basins, dressings, gallon bottles of multicolored pills and capsules lined the wall opposite the bookcase. Filing cases were filled with patients' records. My father's medical history was in that filing cabinet. So was mine. At the far end of the room stood an exercise machine, a heat lamp, a respirator, and a sterilizer. An old walnut office desk and two chairs stood under windows looking out onto the street. I sat on one end of a leather treatment table in the center of the office while Paula piled books on the other end. I was wishing I had gone to San Luis with Hans and Rosamund and Roger.

I stole a quick glance at the books. *The Hindu Art of Love, Sexualis, The Story of Life, Chastity Belts Through the Ages.* The titles gave me goose pimples. Only the day before yesterday I had sat on this same table while Hans removed slivers from my hands. How did I get into this?

"She's probably not ready for the one on frigidity," I heard Paula mutter as she sorted through the books on the table and put a couple back in the bookcase.

Finally, when she had chosen perhaps half a dozen, we crept quietly out of the office and into her parents' bedroom. Paula locked the door and pulled the curtains so Mr. Steffans wouldn't get nosy and then dumped the books on the double bed and turned on the bedside lights. She patted the bed for me to sit beside her.

"Their room is closer to the office in case we have to get these back in a hurry," she explained.

I nodded. Both Paula and I loved to be in this room. The smell of Rosamund's perfume lingered. There was a sumptuousness to the soft apricot and ivory color scheme, and we loved the silkiness of the bedspread, the plumpness of the pillows, the Persian rugs on the floor, her parents clothes in the closet, and the books they were still reading lying open. Besides, it was forbidden territory.

"Come on," Paula repeated.

I hung back. I felt sick to my stomach and yet so curious that my hands were clammy and a flush was spreading over my entire body.

"Oh, come *on*, Anna. You don't want to end up pregnant, do you?"

I shook my head and perched gingerly on the edge of the double bed, my stomach turning somersaults. Suppose I threw up on their bed. Maybe I was already pregnant? Immaculate conception, I thought, deciding that even a poor joke was better than none.

"OK, then, you know that a man and a woman have to mate for her to get pregnant—right?" Though Paula's voice was firm, I noticed that her hands shook.

I had thought mating was a term used for zoo animals, but I nodded. This was no time to interrupt Paula.

"But you don't know quite how they do it, right?" She was rifling through a worn book called *The Story of Life*.

My father had given me this book, without comment, and it left out some vital information about how people mated, though it explained a lot about cows.

"Right," I whispered.

"Like this." And, picking up another book, she showed me. The scientific terms were comforting, but the pictures were beyond belief, and the fear that I still might throw up kept me silent. Paula didn't seem to expect comment.

Then she handed me a huge book called *Sexualis*, and we leafed through photographs of vulvas and breasts of women from around the world. They were so unappetizing I began to calm down. The comparison of penises around the world was sobering too. What I wondered, though, was how the authors got so many people to pose naked? I sure wouldn't. I didn't ask Paula if she would.

I felt a headache coming on and would have given a dollar for a glass of water, but if Paula once stopped reading she probably wouldn't start again, so I didn't say anything.

"So we have to ovulate so the sperm can fertilize the egg, get it?"

I nodded.

"Will you please *say* something?" Paula pleaded.

"Why are—you telling me all this?" I asked.

"Why do you think? So you won't let Big Boy or some other clown get fresh with you, of course."

I remembered the picture of male genitals and attached them to Big Boy and I could hardly breathe.

Then I looked over at Paula, leafing through *The Hindu Art of Love*, and I saw that her face was as red as mine felt. Her hands, holding the book, shook. I looked at the subtitle. A Compendium of Erotic Knowledge of the East with Eighteen Illustrated Coital Positions.

But why was Paula so flushed, so nervous that she was actually shaking? She must have looked at these books a hundred times. It was all new to me, but not to her. She'd only gotten them out this afternoon to protect me. Which was very nice of her. I liked the idea of her protecting me.

So what was the matter with her? She was short of breath, gasping, her chest heaving.

"What are you staring at?" Paula asked sharply.

"What's wrong?"

"What do you mean, what's wrong?" She sounded angry.

"I mean . . . Oh, I don't know." I knew there were tears in my eyes, and crying was the last thing I wanted to do. Who could be so crazy as to burst into tears because of looking at pictures? But they weren't just pictures. They showed what people did. And I didn't want to see and yet my heart was pounding and I did see Big Boy, who was my boss and a married man. Which meant that he and his wife were going all the way. The phrase we used so often to refer to older girls of doubtful reputation came back with illustrations, a kaleidoscope of pictures from the books and visions of people I knew.

"Do you and David go—all the way?" I whispered the question and then wished I hadn't. Paula had just showed me all this—stuff—so I wouldn't get pregnant, and I had no business to pry. But Paula surprised me.

"David?" She asked, rolling her eyes. "He'd faint away dead if he even *saw* one of those illustrations, let alone do anything. David is a rabbit."

"He is—kind of shy," I agreed, thinking of those tender love scenes I had so admired. I felt like a traitor, but I couldn't help understanding what Paula meant. Maybe my old boyfriend and I had the guts, after all. I tried to recall his face, but I couldn't.

"What I'd really like to know . . ." Paula began and then hesitated. "What I'd really like to know is how it feels."

"Paula!"

"Well—if everyone does it eventually, why not?"

I nodded. Why not, really? And suddenly I wanted to know, too. Why did the grown-ups keep it such a secret if sex was so widespread? Locked away. Whispering. "It makes all the grown-ups seem like sneak thieves," I said.

"Hypocrites," Paula replied with a nervous giggle.

"Ridiculous." I giggled, too.

And then we were both giggling and leafing through the books and pointing out penises and vulvas and each picture made us laugh more than the last. Soon we were rolling and laughing, and only when we'd pulled Paula's parents' bedspread off the bed and onto the floor and suddenly heard a rip did we stop. Then we stopped cold.

"Thank God it was only my blouse," Paula said.

She turned her back so I could see the blouse split all the way to her waist.

"Yeah," I replied as we carefully smoothed out the silk bedspread and gathered up the books. I knew what a catastrophe it would have been if we'd ripped the spread, but I didn't want to give Paula a chance to get started on that. We didn't have time. We might never get these books again.

"We'd better put them back in fifteen minutes," Paula said then, checking her watch. She sighed. She must have been thinking the same thing.

And looking at Paula's face, flushed from laughing, it dawned on me that Paula may have looked at these pictures a hundred times, but she'd never had anyone to look at them with her, to talk to. And we had to put them back so soon. Fifteen minutes wasn't long. I started leafing through a book. "Is this what they do when they don't want a baby?" I asked, looking at a picture of a wire mesh basket covering a woman's organs. I couldn't imagine Rosamund wearing one.

"Let me see. No, they use a diaphragm. That's a chastity belt, stupid," Paula replied.

"Oh, sure." I kept leafing through the book while Paula made a hurried trip to the office to replace the other books so that if her parents should come home we wouldn't have them all. She figured that if worst came to worst, she could always hang onto one book until the next time the coast was clear to put it back in the office.

It wasn't a book that her father used very often.

53

She didn't think men locked their wives up into chastity belts anymore. Most of the pictures seemed to be dated several hundred years ago.

Indeed, the various way that men kept their wives' girdles locked so that they could not accept a lover but could go to the bathroom were ingenious. They looked so improbable that they seemed easier—safer—even sexier than the pictures that we might have to deal with. I think Paula and I envied those women, even though we both felt it would be an uncomfortable apparatus to sleep in, even worse than the man in the iron mask. That this was slavery did not occur to me.

By this time curiosity had overcome fear and I asked questions about rusting and blood poisoning and periods and erections, and I discovered that Paula didn't know much more than I did. I think she hoped I might know more than I did. If so, she was disappointed. And I suppose she was, since she kept calling me stupid, but in such a warm, confiding voice that I wasn't insulted.

Too soon we heard the screech of tires hitting gravel in the alley, and Paula ran to replace *Chastity Belts Through the Ages* while I turned off the light and opened the curtains, surprised to find the sun already setting. Mr. Steffans was no longer lying under the zapota tree, and I could smell frying onions as I opened a window toward his house. Paula came back from the kitchen and reported that he'd left a bag of vegetables by our back door.

"I wonder if he heard anything?" I whispered.

"Fortunately, he's hard of hearing," Paula replied. We both blushed.

I happened to know he wasn't too hard of hearing to listen outside Hans's office window because a few days before I'd heard him giving advice. He told Hans he could cure an old man of tuberculosis by getting two pigeon breasts and laying them face down on the man's chest, one over each lung, and leaving them there for three days to pull out the infection. Hans thanked him, but I doubt if he followed his advice. So I knew he could hear, but I wasn't about to tell Paula and scare her to death. "Well, he'd have gotten an earful," was all I'd say.

Paula and I looked at each other and shrugged.

"Mr. Steffans is *such* an old man," Paula said finally.

"Probably impotent," I replied, and was happy to see Paula blush.

6

PAULA'S FACTS OF LIFE lesson left me shaken. I couldn't look at Hans, avoided Mr. Steffans' side of the garden, and even Roger was an embarrassing presence. I would wake in the morning knowing I'd had a nightmare but remembering only being chased by a dark male through the endless halls of a pyramid.

By Monday morning I was grateful enough to go off

to work. It was already hot and muggy as we left the house. Bad business, weather that stills the song of the birds, Mr. Steffans muttered as we passed. And it was true, the squeak of his pump was the only sound carried on the silent air.

"I never thought I'd miss those old roosters," Paula said, looking around nervously.

"Bad business." Mr. Steffans shook his head ominously.

"Earthquake weather," David said when we got to work. "The dog days of August."

We were picking jumbo orange marigolds, and their pungent spicy odor was hypnotic in the still heat. By midmorning I staggered along the row, picking almost at random, not tired so much as rundown.

I can still see Big Boy, tall, and graceful as a leopard, walking toward me between rows of jumbo marigolds. I knew he'd come to teach me how to transplant seedling marigolds. He was smiling, untouched by the heat.

I flushed scarlet and stood up, staring at him, poised to run. I have no idea what I was thinking. Perhaps only that Paula had gotten out the books to warn me about Big Boy, and in some confused way, all my fear and curiosity and longing about sex must have focused on him, so much so that I had to force my eyes up from his fly to his face.

"*Que pasa*, what is wrong, little one?" he asked, and possibly thinking I was ill or feeling my own sensual tension, he reached out to put his hands on my shoulders. There was concern in his brown eyes and, perhaps, a small teasing also.

"Don't you dare touch me, you two-timing bastard!" I hissed. I clapped my hand over my mouth, still staring, appalled. I had never used the word bastard in my whole life before. But I used it then. Paula said later that she heard me from the next row over.

As for Big Boy, his arms dropped as if he'd been burned. He stood there for a moment looking at me, confused at first, and then, as if understanding something, his eyes glinted and I watched the concern and the life fade from them. It was as if his eyes died, and the hazel gleam fading left black. Then a mean look came into his face, and his eyes kept darting around, searching for what? I was terrified, but I couldn't have run, couldn't have screamed, couldn't have moved if my life depended on it. Gradually I realized he was speaking. His voice was quiet and hard, as if he were speaking to himself. But he spoke in English, so I knew he was talking to me.

"I could be deported over this. Only over your talk. Only this. Stay away from me, you. Keep away!" He looked at me a moment more to make sure I understood. Then he turned and walked quickly away, tall and graceful, and only his clenched fists showed anger as he crossed through rows of marigolds, heading for the office.

That was all. When Paula asked what happened, I said we'd seen a rattlesnake. I don't know whether she believed me, but the subject remained closed. Possibly she thought her training had helped me. It didn't seem to matter too much since we would be quitting on Friday, anyhow. The summer was almost over. I remember being relieved that Big Boy would no longer tease me about going to the movies with him. When we left, he said good-bye in a friendly, if offhand, way, and I could almost believe he'd forgotten my words.

Except that in my dreams I would see him, and he was always standing there, virile and teasing, and gradually his eyes would die and as they did, they got bigger and bigger until they were all I could see.

But, if I felt guilty about yelling at Big Boy, the yell itself released something in me, and I was able to look men in the eyes again and laugh with them and go on with life without screaming at every man who laid a hand on my shoulder. I'd let off steam, and I felt myself again. Though that isn't the whole truth. There was a new jauntiness to my walk, a teasing in my glance, lifted eyebrows if I passed an attractive man. There was a new dimension.

And on Sunday we would be leaving for San Francisco with more money than either Paula or I had ever seen, and we could spend every cent on clothing for ourselves. I could buy a whole new wardrobe, and when I came back I would throw away every stitch of the baby clothes I'd been wearing all my life.

The Raymonds were preparing food as if we were going to Europe and had to provision ourselves for six months rather than the one night we planned to spend in San Francisco. I thought it would probably be cheaper to go to Foster's Cafeteria, but I loved popping corn and picking apples and helping Hans knead bread so I didn't say anything. The house was filled with the smells of Rosamund's fudge bars and oatmeal cookies. Roger, though he was staying home with Mr. Steffans to look after the place, claimed he cracked nuts for us eight hours straight and set a record.

At last the great day came, and we left town at dawn, driving north along the coast highway as the sun rose over the blue-gray ocean.

7

IT WAS LATE AFTERNOON when we drove down Market Street toward Powell, five or five-thirty, rush hour. The San Francisco traffic was terrible, bumper-to-bumper, with every car honking and trying to make illegal turns to escape the crush. Above us the tall buildings blocked out the last of the sun, casting a chill gloom over the hurrying crowds.

We were looking for the Powell Hotel, where the Raymonds had stayed before. Somehow, Hans had gotten the idea that this was my hometown and I knew my way around so I was desperately looking for the marquee OWELL. Rosamund had said the P had been burned out last time they were here. Actually, the only times my father and I had come downtown were to attend Sunday matinees at the Fox Theatre or, occasionally, shopping for clothes. Hans undoubtedly knew the city better than I from his annual trips to the Salvation Army and the Goodwill.

"I've never seen so many sourpusses," Paula remarked, looking out the window at the hurrying crowds.

"They're freezing to death in this wind." I defended the people in my city.

"Where do we turn?" asked Hans.

"Oh, look at the man selling newspapers. He's way out in the street. He'll get—"

"Shut up! If you girls aren't going to help—can't you at least keep them quiet, Mother," yelled Hans. For some reason, he was attracting a lot of the honking around us.

"Shhh," said Rosamund.

Then I spied Powell Street. "There it is—Powell—right over there," I yelled exultantly.

"Why didn't you tell me there was no left turn, for Lord sakes? We'll have to go around the block."

We rounded the block and ended up coming back along Powell toward Market because there wasn't a right turn onto Powell at that particular corner. Or perhaps we had been in the wrong lane for a right turn? Hans was used to small-town driving, where there was only one lane in each direction and where everyone gave the doctor the right of way. He was never, Hans yelled, "coming to this demented city again on a fool's errand for a couple of boy-crazy girls who could, just as well, have gotten their clothes at home. Cheaper. Never again, by God. Never, never, never, never, never."

Rosamund said nothing. Paula and I, cowering in the back seat, said nothing either. We all knew that Hans and Rosamund came to the city every fall to shop the Goodwill and Salvation Army for winter clothes, sometimes finding cashmere sweaters and Chinese silk robes, rare books and last year's best-sellers, and that this trip was a high point of the year for both of them.

"It's your fault, you know," Paula whispered.

I knew, all right, I knew to the marrow of my bones. So I glared at her.

"Shut up back there or you'll wish you had," yelled Hans.

Silence.

When she thought it safe, Paula whispered again, more sympathetically. "Do you even know where it is?"

I shook my head, surprised she needed to ask. Even if I *had* known the location of the hotel, which I didn't, once Hans started bellowing my mind blanked out. My heart was pounding. I was drenched in sweat. He'd be sorry if I fainted. Maybe.

Rosamund sat beside Hans, her hands folded in her lap, wearing what Roger called her lunar look. She didn't appear to hear Hans yelling, the traffic honking, nor Paula and I complaining. She didn't appear to be looking for the hotel. I'd seen the same serenely interested look on her face as she watched birds feeding outside the kitchen window at home. Later she could mimic the bird, his song, and his eating habits perfectly. I wondered what she was seeing in the tired people hurrying along the darkening streets beside us. She said nothing, nor did Hans seem to expect her to speak.

Round and round downtown San Francisco we cruised, looking for the Hotel Powell or a gas station or even a policeman. Everywhere we seemed to be in the wrong lane or facing a No Left Turn sign or a One Way Street sign. It was almost dark under the skyscrapers, and it was getting hard to read signs. Hans was worried about running out of gas. I was beginning to recognize the same flower stands and the same restaurants, but I was afraid to tell Hans.

I noticed that Rosamund had put her left hand on Hans's thigh.

"Mother, I don't know where on earth we are," he said wearily.

At that moment the street lights went on, casting a soft glow. There were fewer people now, and they weren't hurrying anymore. The wind had gone down, and the traffic had thinned out. Pedestrians looked happier, and even drivers looked kinder under the lights. You could see diners in the restaurants and flashing neon signs advertised hotels and night life. If only Hans wasn't angry, I would have been content to drive around for hours seeing the city under lights.

"Oh, there it is—over to the left, Daddy, next to the cafeteria," Paula called suddenly. OWELL the sign still read, and we'd missed it because the marquee was around the corner, off Powell, on the other side of the hotel.

"And so the mystery is solved, ladies. How simple it all is when you know where you are in life," Hans said with relief, turning into a garage beneath the hotel.

"Thanks to Paula's sharp eyes," Rosamund added, the first words she'd spoken since we couldn't turn left onto Powell.

"Now I can go to the bathroom," Paula replied, and we all laughed.

"Thank you, Paula," I whispered. "He'd have killed me if we didn't find it soon."

"Hah, now you know how I feel half the time."

I nodded, but we were wrong. For, though I was exhausted and sorry, I did not really know how she felt.

The next morning was the kind of day when country people decide to move to the city. Even downtown we could smell the tang of the ocean. Overhead, sea gulls wheeled in a clear blue sky. The sun was shining, a slight teasing breeze hinted pleasantly of fall, the crowding people were smartly dressed and gave the impression that the errands toward which they were hurrying were important and stimulating. In the sunlight the tall buildings looked imposing, with boxes of blooming chrysanthemums banked against windows filled with elegant fall clothes, and we passed bookstore after bookstore piled high with pyramids of novels I wanted to read.

Hans stopped at a flower stand and bought us each

a gardenia corsage, my first corsage, and I couldn't smell it enough. We went on down the block to a Foster's Cafeteria where everyone ordered breakfast, the first time I had eaten breakfast in a restaurant. I found it almost impossible to choose between pancakes with scrambled eggs and french toast with fresh strawberries. Finally I chose the french toast because it seemed more cosmopolitan, more what a young woman wearing a gardenia would choose, and then watched with greedy envy while Paula poured syrup over her pancakes. She used the entire pitcher all by herself.

After breakfast, Rosamund and Hans walked Paula and me over to the Emporium, where we were to shop while they spent the morning at the nearby Goodwill and Salvation Army, buying winter clothes and the luxuries that made these trips such treasure hunts. The plan was that Paula and I would choose what we liked, and then Rosamund would help us make the final selections when we met again under the big clock at noon.

Once again, Hans thought I must know this city. This time he put Paula in my charge on the assumption that I knew the layout of the store. Once again I knew nothing and hadn't the guts to say so. So I stood under the Emporium clock watching Hans and Rosamund walk away. I saw Hans take Rosamund's hand, and then she gave a little skip to catch up with him, something girlish I'd never seen her do before. Neither of them looked back. They're escaping, I thought, forgetting that when Rosamund had asked if we wanted her to stay with us, Paula and I had both accused her of treating us like babies.

"Well," Paula said when they were out of sight. "I don't suppose you know where anything is here, either, right?"

"You know something, Paula. You have a definite tendency to martyrdom," I said. "No, I don't know here, either." I felt better, relieved of responsibility. Let Paula figure it out.

Paula, who had never been to San Francisco before, let alone a big department store, gave me a withering look and walked over to an information booth I hadn't noticed and had the woman write out directions to the departments we wanted. They talked for several minutes first, and I decided that if I ever went around the world, I'd invite Paula to come along.

"You're such a nearsighted old cow," Paula said cheerfully when she returned, and I followed her without the dignity of an answer.

We soon settled on the basement because checking price tags we learned we didn't have as much money as we'd thought we had. We could get more for our money downstairs. Rosamund had suggested we try for a couple of skirts and sweaters, or a suit, a good dress and a pair of pants. But it was up to us. "It's your money, have a fling," she'd said. "Just don't forget school shoes."

I stood looking at the long racks of clothes with

determined women sorting through them. I was bewildered. But Paula started down the aisles as if she were born to shopping. I had usually gone shopping each school term with my father, and he had made most of the selections, though I'd had veto power. Maybe I should wait until Rosamund came back.

A young saleswoman who looked a little like Judy Garland came over and asked if I could use some help. Gratefully, I surrendered myself to her taste.

The first thing she brought was a tissue green wool suit with clear plastic buttons centered in gold rosebuds. The suit fit like a glove and, looking in the mirror, I felt I'd become a woman. I was seeing *myself* for the first time.

"Fits you to a T, it does. I tried it on myself and it was too tight for me, but you've the figure for it all right," said the saleswoman, moving about so she could judge the suit from different angles.

"You'll have to change the buttons," said Paula.

"But you like it?" I asked. I would never change the buttons.

"It's not what kids wear to school, but it looks good on you, and with simpler buttons, you could get by. But try on some others—that's the first thing you've tried on—"

"But you like it?" I persisted.

"Well—it's all right. How much does it cost?"

"I'll take it. Wrap it up," I said to the clerk. What

was the use of trying another suit when this was made for me. As for the price, I would gladly have worked all summer just for that suit, but miraculously, it took less than half what I had to spend.

"It's a good buy. *And* a smart shopper who knows what she wants right off. You should see some of 'em." The clerk shook her head sadly before going off with my suit. I hated to let it out of my sight.

"We're supposed to wait for Mother before buying," Paula said doubtfully.

"It's my business."

"I guess . . ." Paula had tried on half a dozen suits and was trying on a beige tweed for the second time. She adjusted the three way mirror so that she could see how she looked from every angle. It fit well, made her look like Greer Garson, but who wanted to look like a middle-aged Englishwoman? I could tell that Paula liked the suit, and maybe, with a red sweater, it would do. I waited for Paula to ask what I thought, but she still hadn't when the salesgirl came back with my suit.

"*That's* quality, *that* suit is," the girl said to Paula, handing me my suit box with a brief smile of dismissal. I decided she didn't look nearly so much like Judy Garland as I'd thought. Buck teeth, for one thing.

By the time we left that clerk, we'd each chosen a sweater and skirt as well as our suits and I was feeling lightheaded. I wanted to skip through the store, pulling clothes off the rack and trying them on for the sheer joy of seeing myself a woman instead of a kid. I felt like Venus rising from the sea, unveiled rather than hidden by my new clothes.

"You spend money like it's going out of style," Paula said. "Don't forget you need shoes."

"Sure, don't worry," I said, thinking about a tiger-striped dress I'd seen on a dummy. It was on sale, and I was afraid it would be sold if I didn't hurry back. "You go on, and I'll catch up with you," I added.

Paula looked dubious but finally turned and headed for the shoes. Paula loved shoes passionately and always had, and she was seldom satisfied with the compromises she and her mother reached when they bought together. I knew this was her one chance.

By the time we met Rosamund and Hans under the Emporium clock, both Paula and I had spent all our money, and neither of us wanted Rosamund to check our purchases. I couldn't remember ever being so happy.

"Well, girls," said Rosamund, smiling. "You must have bought out the store."

"Couldn't. We ran out of money."

"Let's take a look," Rosamund suggested. "Daddy is going to take us to Golden Gate Park for a picnic when we're through."

"We're through. Let's go," Paula and I insisted in unison.

"But it will be such a nuisance to send things back later if you decided you don't like something," Rosamund began uncertainly.

I knew my tiger-striped dress couldn't be returned since it was on sale.

"It's our money." Paula sounded a little defensive. I couldn't think why. Only a mother could love that tweed suit, and Paula hadn't seen my tiger dress yet.

"Well, let's not stand here all day, girls."

"Anna? Are you sure your clothes will be all right for our hick town?" Rosamund asked dubiously.

"Oh, yes, I love my clothes. Paula helped me."

"Mother!"

"Well, it *is* their money . . ." Rosamund appealed to Hans.

He shrugged.

We stood in an island with shoppers hurrying around us, bumping and then gliding off, as if we were rocks and they were carried along in the current. I held my breath, suddenly *sure* there would be trouble if Rosamund saw my tiger dress. Please, I prayed silently.

"Shall we go?" Hans asked. "We are on a holiday."

Reluctantly, slowly, Rosamund looked up at him and smiled. She seemed to be thinking something through. "Oh, I suppose I am being a mother hen. If you girls are old enough to earn your own money, you should be old enough to spend it. Just so long as you realize we can't afford to buy you more clothes for school."

"I wouldn't even wear anything you'd buy. Now, let's go," Paula said.

Hooray, hooray, hooray! I wanted to shout as we

turned and left the store with our packages safely in our arms, but I restrained myself. Paula winked at me behind her mother's back. We'd won and we knew enough to be quiet.

It was one of those balmy September days that have given San Francisco its reputation, and Hans talked all the way to Golden Gate Park about how lucky my father and I had been to live there. Hans was always wistful about cities where a doctor didn't have to be on call night and day for every emergency and baby delivery, where he wouldn't have to tend his friends when they died, where he could earn a decent living and take a week at a time for vacation. Where he wouldn't have such a big garden to tend. Rosamund said he'd go stir-crazy if he wasn't the big cheese in town, and he'd wither away without roses to baby; and all of us, including Hans, knew she was right. Furthermore, I could have told him we'd spent our two years holed up in a three-room apartment in the ash gray Richmond district. I walked two blocks to the library, three blocks to a second-hand, funny book store, and twelve blocks to school, and that was my San Francisco.

"My father always said S.F. was good for *tourists*," I muttered. "But I can show you a great place in the park for lunch—Stowe Lake."

My sense of direction isn't good even when I know where I'm going, but this was a charmed day and a few minutes later we were parked by the grassy side of the lake, pestered by mallards who were mad for our left-over popcorn. Two swans swam placidly on the lake, ignoring us. Rosamund said she thought swans might be insect eaters and choosy at that.

We ate the last of our food from home: Tillamook cheese sandwiches, our first Gravenstein apples, and brownies. Roger's nuts were a particular pleasure since we usually had to crack our own.

Hans had hauled a Chinese chest the size of a small hope chest up on the bank and after lunch painted it with a solvent to dissolve at least fifty years' accumulation of grease. This was his great find from the Goodwill. It turned out to be rosewood outside and cedar within and delicately carved. The front panel showed a family having tea: a mother and a father, grandparents, and three children, two girls about ten and a small boy. A weeping willow framed an oval around the panel. Just like us, I thought. I kept hoping someone else would notice the similarity. I wanted to hear it, but if I said anything it would be like begging.

"Who on earth would have thrown *that* away?" Paula asked. "You found a masterpiece, Daddy."

"Probably some sailor kept everything he owned in the world inside that chest, and when he died the captain gave it to the Goodwill. I've heard they do that," Hans answered, smiling at Paula. Her compliments were rare.

"I wonder," Rosamund said, "if this is the carver's

family or maybe the family of the man who commissioned the chest. They look like faces he was familiar with."

"I feel as if I know them," I said.

"Such a patient face on that woman," Rosamund murmured, and I wondered if she identified with the mother.

"My mother had a face like that," Hans said. "Did you know my mother was an opera singer, Annie? Well, she was, and when she practiced she always had the window open so she could see the linden tree in our garden, summer and winter. In Austria we lived then. That woman must have loved her willow like my mother loved that linden tree. My father used to say she'd catch her death of pneumonia, but she had to have that window open when she practiced." Hans's face glowed as he shared his memory.

"How did your mother feel about roses?" Rosamund asked with a smile. I realized Rosamund had been remembering something too when she looked at the carving, but Rosamund was not such a memory-sharer, and we would probably never know what she saw.

"Couldn't bear any plant with a thorn, said my father was thorny enough for a lifetime," Hans answered, and we all laughed.

"Runs in the family, then."

"Mother, you're terrible!" Paula clapped her hands in delight.

I loved to watch Hans when Rosamund teased him.

Such a look of wondering gaiety came over his face, even when the joke was on him. Rosamund was a quiet woman, and her wit always seemed to come as a bonus to Hans.

A faint breeze rustled the trees behind us and rippled the still lake, reminding us that we would be leaving soon, and we grew quiet. It would be hard to leave the warm sun and our rare holiday.

Too soon, Hans told us to climb in. Paula and I sat in the back of the car, our packages stored in the Chinese chest. We were content to let Hans and Rosamund talk quietly in the front, while we dozed, dreaming of our new clothes.

The sky was already coloring as we left the park and turned toward the beach, intending to drive along the coast until dark. And then a small thing happened, so small it should not be worth mentioning. It was only this, that Hans thought I would enjoy driving by the apartment house where my father and I had lived. I protested in vain. Hans was not capable of imagining that I did not love that apartment as he loved *every* home in which he had ever lived.

So, once again we turned off Geary Avenue down the block toward the large, square, buff stucco apartment building I used to call the cell block. The bells from the Catholic church on the corner were chiming, and old ladies in black climbed up the steep marble stairs as we passed, but in the block where I had lived there was not one person on the street. There had seldom been evidence that people lived behind those closed windows. Nothing had altered on that block, though my whole life had changed in the four months since I had left.

One shade was up in our corner apartment, and through the voile curtains, I saw again an emaciated old Boston fern in a particularly ugly pot-metal stand. It had been my job to water that fern, and I had even bought fertilizer out of my allowance, hoping to help the fern look like its relatives in flower shops. But no such luck. Nor had it improved over the summer. Suddenly I thought of what Hans had said about some patients being endurers. That fern was an endurer, waiting for me to come back, knowing I could not escape that dark apartment any more than it could. It was our fate. This feeling of inevitability was so strong that my teeth were chattering and I could only nod when Hans pointed out the apartment.

8

It was well after midnight before we reached home, and Rosamund told us to sleep in the following morning. This was a rare treat, so I was startled to find Paula at my door while I could still see the morning star on the dark horizon. She carried a shoebox under her arm and looked worried.

"We don't have to work today," I said.

"Shhhhh," she hissed, so like a melodrama heroine that I laughed.

"Shut up, will you? It isn't funny." And by this time I could see tears in her eyes.

"Come on in," I said and shut the door behind us.

"If my parents ever find out how much I spent for these shoes they'll scratch my eyes out."

"It's your money, isn't it? Didn't Rosamund say it was our money?" I asked. "My father never asked what I did with my money."

Paula, it turned out, had bought a pair of shoes that cost as much as my father spent to board me a whole month, as much as the Raymonds had spent for all of Roger's school clothes. I'd never seen such expensive shoes before, and I was curious about that shoebox Paula kept stroking as she sat on the edge of my bed.

"Let's see."

"We have to burn the sales receipts—now—and then keep them from seeing our clothes as long as we can. I've been up all night thinking, and that's the only way," Paula talked on and on as if she couldn't stop.

"Let's see them."

"Have you heard a single word I said? No, don't turn on the light. Daddy might get up and see it. Leave it off."

I sighed. If Paula bought a hamburger, it was a secret.

"OK, OK. I'll say I have to go to the library today. Now, let's see those shoes."

"It'll take more than the library," Paula muttered, but her face brightened as she undid the string around the box, lifted the lid, and placed an ordinary moccasin on her palm. "They're *I. Miller's*," she whispered.

"They look as if they'll last," I muttered. Brown moccasins were *all* they were. She'd been gypped. I hunted around for something nice to say, and all the time she was holding those shoes as if they were Cinderella's glass slippers. Paula didn't even notice my silence. She didn't need my approval.

"See the double stitching. Hand rolled. They'll last clear through school, the man said."

I let her stare at them awhile, and then I brought up the subject of burning those sales slips before Hans had to go out on an early morning house call or something. Paula was all business at that and took a box of wooden matches and her sales receipts out of her sweater pocket. I dumped mine out of the bags and didn't stop for more than a quick, satisfying look at my new clothes.

We headed through the vegetable garden for the incinerator near Mr. Steffans's yard. We hadn't gotten far before we thought we heard voices. We stopped and looked around but couldn't see anything through the fog. We listened but heard nothing more. Then a foghorn moaned offshore, and we giggled. Probably only the wind. Still, we waited, as Hans had been robbed of drugs twice, and we didn't want to surprise any burglars.

Next I heard a strange scratching sound, like digging. I looked at Paula, and she nodded.

"Over to the left," she said, indicating Mr. Steffans's place.

Stealthily, we crept toward the sound, careful to keep out of sight, stopping behind the persimmon tree. As the fog lifted a little, we saw Mr. Steffans directing Roger, who was digging a deep hole.

"What on earth—" Paula never finished her sentence. We were both too busy watching Mr. Steffans sitting on the cold sand counting greenbacks into a Mason jar.

"How much?" Roger asked.

"Two hundred and eighty dollars," Mr. Steffans replied, screwing on the lid, checking to make sure it was tight.

"With the other jars that tops six hundred dollars," Roger said.

"It's like pirates," I whispered.

"Shhhh."

Roger grunted, lowering the jar gently into the hole and filling the hole quickly with sand. Then Roger swept dirt over the spot, placed a eucalyptus stump directly on top, and sat down, smiling.

Only when Roger finished did the old man finally speak. His voice had a dignity in the chill dawn.

"If God grants, I shall see my mother and my brothers once again," he said and shook Roger's hand. Roger's smile was wonderful. Then the old man put an arm around his shoulder, and they strode off toward Mr. Steffans's house.

Paula and I looked at each other.

"What's all the buried money about?" I asked as Paula stuffed our sales slips in the incinerator and lit a match to them.

"There—before someone else comes by. How should I know? And Roger will never spill the beans. He's got this thing about secrecy. But Mr. S. is always talking about going back to Crete and saving his relatives from the Germans.

"But in a Mason jar?" I thought Roger wasn't the only one with a thing about secrecy.

Paula shrugged. "I heard he lost money in the Depression." Paula seemed sad. This was one more secret in Roger's life, one more time he didn't need her.

I could see smoke coming out of Mr. Steffans's chimney, swirling through the Belle of Portugal roses like fog. I could smell cocoa and frying vegetables. It would be warm in there, and I was hungry. Suddenly it wasn't only that I had to find out what they were doing with the money jars. I wanted to tell Mr. Steffans and Roger about our trip to San Francisco. I'd steered clear of his house, but this morning it seemed cozy, familiar.

"We could go knock on his door, and I bet he'd make us breakfast too," I said eagerly.

"No, we could *not*," Paula replied firmly. "You really have to learn to mind your own business, Anna.

Roger has a right to his own life. Besides, suppose they ask what we were doing out here at dawn?"

We could tell them, I thought, but I shrugged and followed her back to my room, stopping to pick an apple and an avocado on the way. The fog was lifting, and it was going to be a still, warm day. It always was when the surf was so loud in summer.

"You've got to help me convince them," Paula was saying.

I was uneasy about how *they'd* like my tiger dress, so I kept repeating what Rosamund had said about having the right to spend what we earned. "Roger always says the best thing with your mother is to face her and get it over with."

"How about Daddy?"

"He could care less. He doesn't know one shoe from another."

"You promise you won't tell what they cost?"

I was getting bored. "Scout's honor. Anything you bring out I'll say is grand, and anything I bring out, you say it's just what everyone wears at your school. Regardless. Right? Come on Paula, you've burned the price tag. Relax!"

Paula turned on me, then. "Don't you ever tell me to relax again! You're always telling me to relax lately, and I hate it! Hate it!" Paula shouted, hands on her hips.

I wonder why, I thought, but I kept my mouth shut. Maybe Paula had a shoe fetish, but who cared?

Her shoes had cost more than my green suit so they must be important, but she didn't have to ruin the day over them.

"You just don't understand," she said and darted out of the room, leaving me free to try on my new clothes and wonder why Mr. S. buried his money in Mason jars.

We were all tired that night when we finally brought in our new clothes to model for Hans, Rosamund, and Roger. As Hans said, that had been *some* twenty-four hours in the big City. The Raymonds' living room smelled of incense, and candles cast a soft glow over everything. I could tell Hans and Rosamund wanted to get our fashion show over so they could go to bed and read.

They liked Paula's suit and that got us off to a good start. Hans said my suit looked more like a costume than school clothes, but he liked the color and Rosamund suggested I change the buttons. Rosamund's opinion meant a lot to me and I didn't like the resignation in her voice, but at least I could keep the suit.

Then I put on my jersey tiger dress, and Paula brought out her shoes.

"Oh, no," said Rosamund, looking at the *I. Miller* label inside Paula's moccasins.

"Better send that back, honey," Hans said, looking at me in the dress.

"I can't. The dress was on sale. A great sale— under ten dollars."

"Ten bucks down the drain. You'll never wear it."

Wait and see, I thought. Just wait and see. Fortunately, Rosamund was in shock over the price of Paula's shoes, even though Paula had cut the price in half for the occasion. She didn't even look at my dress, and I hurried out to change before she did.

"Must be the inflation," Paula was saying, her voice a whisper, as I returned.

"They're nice shoes, Paula—soft and sensible for school but . . ."

"It's Paula's money," I said, safe since I'd changed out of the tiger dress. "You *said* if we earned it—"

"Yes, yes, I know. I wanted you girls to make your own decisions—and they will last a long while . . ." Rosamund turned to Hans, and they shrugged at each other. "But neither your father nor I have ever spent so much on a pair of shoes."

"As long as she doesn't expect us to buy her clothes . . ." Hans left the sentence unfinished.

Then Paula assured them she wouldn't need another thing and brought out her other skirt and sweater as proof. The storm was wearing down. I envied Paula her parents total concern over her shoes. There would have been much more fuss over the tiger dress if it had been Paula's dress, I thought. Still, our sticking together *had* pulled us through.

Unfortunately, school started the following week and we started drifting apart. On the surface we were close enough. I ate lunch with Paula and her friends.

We saved each other places in the bus line when David wasn't taking Paula home. But he took her home more and more often, and finally they began eating lunch by themselves. David and Paula became one of the school couples, and increasingly, they kept to themselves.

We drifted but the only real trouble between us came over Paula's geometry lessons.

They began a week after school started. Paula had flunked her first exam. Math and science were difficult for Paula, and she needed good grades to get into nursing school. She'd had trouble in algebra the year before and had struggled to make a C. Therefore, after the first geometry exam, she asked her mother for help. Rosamund looked over her text and asked Hans to refresh her memory on some point. Instead, Hans put down his cello.

When Hans stood up, Paula froze. The color drained from her face, reinforcing a silence so sudden the strains of cello music seemed to hang in the air, still vibrating.

Hans may have felt this too, for he sighed as he slid in behind the red oilcloth covering the kitchen table, moving over next to Paula, snapping off the portable radio at her side. On the divider was a bud vase with a single yellow rose, and Hans reached up and smelled the rose. In the silence I could hear the vase scraping a little as he set it back on the shelf. Then there was only the crackle of green eucalyptus wood popping in the fireplace.

I must have been staring again, for I looked up and found Rosamund looking at me, a curious, measuring look. Not unfriendly, but impersonal and evaluating. Possibly she wondered what I was thinking. I was thinking she would never have looked at her daughter that way. She cast that look on a patient sometimes when she wasn't sure she believed his story. But I hadn't said a word, so what did she want from me?

I would never know, for just at that moment Hans called.

"Annie," he asked in a tired voice. "Annie, do you need help too?"

"She's only in algebra," Paula said, and I could not tell whether she wished I was going to be included or not.

"I could help her next. How did you do in the first test, Annie?" Hans turned to me, persisting.

"A."

"The San Francisco schools are ahead. She'd already had some." There was a curious pleading in Paula's voice.

"Always excuses," Hans snapped and turned to read over the lesson.

"I couldn't remember how you come by the proofs," Rosamund said. "I can help her if you'll just show me."

"That's because this is such a stupid way of demonstrating a theorem," Hans said, and then he proceeded to show us all a simpler way. It made sense. I could follow even without having had geometry.

"Do you get it, honey?"

"It doesn't matter whether I do or not," Paula replied in the same weary tone Hans had used. "They want us to do it *their* way. *Mother*. Tell him they want the geometry proved their way. Tell him!"

We all looked at Rosamund.

"That's true," she said so quietly we could hardly hear her.

"Just do it this way once and see if it doesn't work," Hans insisted, ignoring Rosamund's comment.

"Mother!" Paula demanded.

Rosamund said nothing.

"They didn't accept your way of doing the problems last year in algebra. That's why I got a C."

"That's not why you got a C."

"It is. It is. And my algebra teacher told my geometry teacher about you."

"Crazy old maid." Hans flushed.

"Mother, help me. *Make* him do it their way. He can. Please."

This time both Paula and Hans looked to Rosamund. And both seemed to be asking her for more than the method of proving a theorem. They were asking her to choose between them.

No one had asked me a thing, so why did I open my big mouth? Was I already so jealous? Did I have to be part of every family scene? I do not know, but I should have been quiet that one time in my life.

"Hans's way really does make more sense. Look,

he cuts out half the steps and makes it so plain," was what I said.

"See, Annie's got a head on her shoulders. She *can* think. And *she* hasn't even had geometry," Hans said, turning on Paula, and I knew I'd made a mistake.

"So how does she know? Of course, it makes sense to her," Paula growled. "Anything you say makes sense to *her*."

"Why *not* just do it by book even if it's a little silly, Hans," Rosamund suggested.

"Because it's unnecessary, that's why, Mother. Your daughter wants to be a nurse. She'd be a good nurse. She has no head for math. Well, you know you don't, Paula. Do it my way."

Then Paula must have either made a face or Hans thought she did.

Hans pushed himself up and leaned on the table. "If I had made a face like that, my father would have knocked me across the room." He struggled to control himself, and I could see his face gradually drain of the purple flush.

Paula stood her ground, biting her lip. "They don't care what's right or easier. They want it their way. And I have to get a B for entrance requirements. It's as simple as that."

They glared at each other. Silently Hans sat down and worked out the first two theorems for Paula, his way, while she sat motionless by his side. She hardly seemed to be listening.

"There," Hans said, calmer now.

"It's nine-thirty already," Paula replied.

"Show me how it's done," Hans said then, taking away the paper.

"Anna, go do your homework in your own room," Rosamund ordered. She'd never ordered me before. As I jumped up and sidled out, I could see Paula twiddling with her pencil while she read over the first problem.

Hans looked ready to pounce. He must have seen that she hadn't been listening.

I could hear them arguing another half-hour, than Paula crying, then silence.

This scene went on twice a week all that fall. It got so that if Paula got out her geometry homework on the kitchen table, Rosamund, Roger, and I *all* left the room. Why Paula continued to do her homework in the kitchen and to ask for help is beyond me. Nor do I understand why Hans continued to insist on his techniques after the teachers marked Paula down. But neither of them gave in. As I wrote my father, they were the two most stubborn people I'd ever met; neither one would give an inch, and the Lord only knew how it would all end.

9

FALL WAS PARTICULARLY BEAUTIFUL that year. Day after day of early morning frost followed by balmy afternoons turned willows golden and oaks a translucent red. And the October winds failed to arrive so the colors held, dotting the green and tawny fields of our beach town with New England color. The skies were so clear and the air so still that I could open my door and hear the wild surf pounding even as I smelled the roses in Hans's garden. And how those roses bloomed. Hans filled the house to asphyxiation with them, as Rosamund said. Every patient carried away roses. At night I dropped off to sleep, drugged by their perfume.

After such hopes and fears, I found school pleasantly dim, which suited me. I was content to eat with Paula's friends and enjoy the appearance of popularity that came from being seen with upper classmen. I had moved with my father enough to know that it takes a year or so to make a good friend in a new school, so I did not hurry. It was enough that for the first time in my life I was considered a pretty girl. More than enough. And I had Paula, when she wasn't off with David.

And, at home, I had Roger. For if the geometry lessons drove a wedge between Paula and me, they gradually forced Roger and me into a conspiracy. Paula was so furious that we seemed to make good grades without visible effort that we each went out of our way to prove her right. One night Roger admitted studying on the sly to "get Paula's goat." So I told him about studying in bed and shoving my algebra papers under the covers when Paula came in, pretending I'd been reading a novel.

87

I had not been given to duplicity before, but there was something about being accused of brains that made me want to live up to the insult, especially since I had already learned that if good grades were a disgrace in our high school, and they were, then studying to make those grades was despicable. In Roger's case, feminine; in mine, unfeminine. In either case, the best way to become an instant wallflower.

For the first time in my life I was not a wallflower, and I had no intention of reverting, certainly not for the love of algebra. Paula could afford to study, since she was the prettiest girl in school, had a steady boyfriend on the basketball team, and the excuse of needing grades because she wanted to be a nurse. My only ambition was to be anonymously popular.

In fact, I went from duplicity to outright lying that fall. Paula and David had been making money on the side, accompanying at dances and at churches, with Paula on the piano and Dave on his guitar or sax. The accompanying had been Paula's idea, and it was a lot more profitable than working in the garden as Roger and I were doing. But being in business together started them fighting. When they'd had a fight, Paula would have me get on the phone and tell David she was busy when she wasn't doing a thing except crying over him. I had never lied before and was rather surprised to find what an exciting game it became. Even though I liked David a lot, I got so I could lie Paula out of the house for three days at a time and have a great time doing it.

It was one of the things that made me wonder about myself that fall. At the rate I was going, I'd be forging checks before I was eighteen.

Meanwhile, I had begun dating myself, though no one as interesting as David. While it is true that I'd had this French-kissing boyfriend to whom I had written pages filled with the single word *love*, I had never had a *date* before coming to live with the Raymonds. That is, a boy who said he was coming to pick me up and take me to a specific place: the movies, a dance, a class picnic, bowling, or a birthday party. These boys came to the front door, and Rosamund answered as she would for a patient since all *their* friends came to the back door. Then she left the date in the waiting room as if he were a patient, and the boys were so terrified they would dare other boys to date us and go through the waiting room initiation. *This* may even have been the secret of my sudden popularity.

At any rate, on one particularly balmy October night I was going to a school dance with a boy named Johnny Wilson, a mild boy with an occasional mean streak, who played second-string football and worked on his father's ranch, one of the largest ranches in South County. We had nothing in common that I could discover, so I was particularly flattered about this date. He was popular with everyone, and he was sitting in Dr. Raymond's waiting room because he wanted to go out with me. I could hear Johnny clear his throat.

"Friday night, and Annie's going out again. Those

boys must think you're in heat," Hans said. We were still at dinner, and I was being held prisoner until I finished the food on my plate. Paula had a job that night and had already left. I was neither insulted nor shocked by Hans's comment, which simply came from being a country doctor. I liked to think I was so sexy no one could resist me. I waited to see if Hans would do what he often did, line up the wine bottles and say that once those hormones got going they just flowed from one bottle to the other and there wasn't a thing in this world that could stop them. I was a little disappointed when he went on eating.

"They think she's a good listener," Roger said. I suppose they did since he usually reported straight facts.

Hans accepted this, too, and was silent for a moment, possibly listening to the polka on the phonograph. "Well, who is it this time, Mother?" he asked finally.

Rosamund turned to me. I'd told her. Each date had to pass Rosamund, a formality since she wasn't given to vetoes. Besides, telling her was an acceptable way of bragging.

"Don't forget he's in the waiting room listening to every word you say," I whispered.

I waited, raising an eyebrow. It sometimes took her a while, but Rosamund always remembered our dates, rehearsals, dental appointments, test scores, end of report periods, ex-friends, and current friends, the thousand and one items of interest to each of us. It was the most reliable and amazing aspect of being part of a family, this motherly interest in *anything* that concerned me. But each time, I had a small catch of fear. Perhaps she would not remember this time. After all, I wasn't Paula or Roger.

"Oh, yes," she said finally, a smile playing around the corners of her mouth. "It's the little Wilson boy. You know Hans, the youngest one, the one with the bad mastoid year before last. February."

Then it was Hans's turn to consider, to go back through the filing cabinet in his memory. He sipped his wine speculatively, separating the Wilsons from the Garcias and the Grenmans, remembering by illness.

"She's not dating one of *those* Wilsons? Out Marinero Road?" he said finally, frowning.

Dating one of the Wilsons meant I was accepted by the most important crowd in school. That was the best thing about Johnny, I thought.

"That's the grandfather," Rosamund replied easily.

Hans spoke in his normal voice, just under a roar. "That family's riddled with syphilis. She'd better get rid of *that* kid."

"Shhh," Rosamund said.

"Men in that family even took it home to their wives. Lord, what a mess that was," Hans continued.

Roger slipped out from the table and turned up the phonograph.

I flushed as scarlet as if I'd been living with Johnny rather than dating him for the first time. I'd never have to worry about getting rid of him. He'd dump *me*. That was certain, and I'd be fortunate if he didn't do something nasty, as well. Like saying I'd gone all the way with him.

"We're only going to a dance," I hissed, finishing artichokes, which I loathed. I had to get out of there before Hans could say anything else. I slipped from the table and headed for my coat, wishing I could faint or come down with a sudden flu, anything to avoid spending an evening with a guy who had just heard that his family was riddled with syphilis.

"Well, be sure to wash your hands after you touch his, before you eat anything, Honey," Hans said as I put on my coat. His eyes were concerned, and I felt momentarily important.

"Hans, you really should be more discreet," Rosamund said softly.

"Mother, we're responsible for that girl."

I took a deep breath and opened the door to the waiting room and faced Johnny. One look at his flushed face, and I knew he'd heard us.

"Well?" I asked, ready to call off the date.

He jerked his head toward the front door. "Let's go," he said.

That was the last word either of us spoke until we reached the dance. I'm not sure we spoke again all evening. We danced together, as stiff as two-by-fours, each relieved when someone else cut in. It did not occur to either of us that we might talk about what he'd overheard. Johnny might have been comforted to hear that the news made his family more interesting; but I was frightened and said nothing. Nor did either of us have the wit to claim a headache. We were condemned by our embarrassment to spend that miserable evening together. Condemned because we were both afraid to admit we'd heard Hans's words.

Curiously, I did not feel particularly sorry for Johnny. I did wonder what he'd tell the other boys. Not the truth, I was sure.

Johnny never asked me out again. For the rest of our time in high school, I would flush slightly if I saw him, and I think he went out of his way to avoid me. When we were forced to meet at a party, we were hearty in our greeting and then got out of each other's way. He must not have said anything at home, for his family all continued to be patients and Hans treated Johnny himself for pneumonia two months later. I never mentioned the episode because I had seen the concern in Hans's eyes and that was what mattered to me.

10

BY NOVEMBER OF 1942 the war was beginning to involve South County. The dressmaker's son, killed in action, was buried with full military honors. There were more servicemen on the streets. But for me, so far, the war had meant my father's letters, first from basic training and then from England, and he wrote more about relatives he was seeing (whom I would try to separate out in dim snapshots) than he did about bombings. We listened to Edward R. Murrow on the six o'clock news, but to me, at fourteen, he sounded like the *March of Time* newsreels of war we'd been seeing for years. I knew this was worse, "our world at war," but I felt little. There were the servicemen on the streets—tanned and muscular and smiling—and we knew they would be shipped overseas from Camp San Luis or Camp Roberts nearby. They might never come back, and so they were out for a good time and couldn't worry about the consequences to the girl, so we had to watch ourselves, Hans said. No dating servicemen.

Then one Monday afternoon in late November, the principal called me out of English and asked if I would like to help sell War Bonds. One girl was being chosen from each grade for beauty, brains, and the ability to sell bonds, he said. The following Saturday we four would rumble through the Arroyo-Pismo valley in Army tanks publicizing the War Bond effort. We would stop at every post office and sell bonds.

I hardly heard beyond the word tanks. I wanted to go, I wanted to go more desperately than I'd ever wanted anything, and I knew Hans would hate it, would say it was the worst idea he'd ever heard. No, no, no, he'd say. For once, I wished my father were home. He'd let me go, he'd let me because it was helping the war effort. Besides, he had faith in me. He didn't think I was going to come home from every date with syphilis.

I didn't let the fact that I had never had a date, let alone a chance to ride around in a tank when I lived with him, confuse the issue. Hans just didn't trust me.

"Oh, I'd love to. Could you—please—ask Dr. Raymond for me?"

The principal hesitated. I wondered if Hans were his doctor. Or maybe he'd heard about the geometry lessons. Or maybe he thought I was on restriction.

"Please. My dad's in the Army so I really need to sell bonds." What I needed was to ride around town in a tank with guns sticking out the turret, but the principal couldn't be sure of that. This was early in the war and not many high school girls' fathers were in the service yet. This principal was a mild, good man. A timid man. He was caught.

"I'll try," was the most he would promise. "Maybe it would be better to keep this our secret for the time being."

My heart sank. He was sorry he'd asked me. Nevertheless, I agreed and got through the day without telling anyone, even Paula. I am not good at keeping secrets, and this was the most important thing that had ever happened to me. This was my own triumph. I wasn't being chosen as Paula's substitute. I wanted everyone to know even if I couldn't go. They'd know *I* had been chosen.

Still, I didn't tell. Not out of sympathy for the girl who would go in my place. A sock in the jaw was good enough for her. I suppose, I appreciated Hans worrying about me, and I didn't want other kids thinking he was cruel if he didn't let me go. He might be wrong, but he wasn't cruel.

It was an overcast day, and the wind tore at me as I struggled home from the bus stop that afternoon. Winter would be closing in soon. Paula and I trudged along without speaking. I do not know what Paula was thinking, but I was possessed by hope and by dread. Probably Hans and Rosamund had already decided whether I could go or not. I'd know the minute I saw them. I'd see it in their faces.

So I pushed past Paula into the house. The kitchen and living room were warm and smelled of the eucalyptus wood crackling in the fireplace. Rosamund sat at the mangle in the living room, ironing. After a moment I caught the steamy smell of freshly ironed clothes. Rosamund looked up, her face showing nothing but pleasure to see us. Inscrutable as Charlie Chan, Roger said of his mother's face.

"Hi," I said, my heart sinking.

"Hello, Mother," Paula called from the kitchen.

"Hello, you two. Have a good day? Mr. Steffans brought over some pomegranates from his tree."

I shrugged, watching Paula grab a pomegranate, sniff it, and take it along as she went downstairs to practice piano. Rosamund went back to her ironing. When Paula's footsteps on the stairs ceased, there was no sound except the crackling fire and the purr of the mangle, punctuated by the click of the release lever from time to time. Hans must be in the office with a patient. Maybe he hadn't told Rosamund yet. He'd simply said no. Or maybe the principal hadn't worked up the courage to call yet. That was more likely since Hans would have come storming in first thing to complain to Rosamund. Somehow, I couldn't bring myself to ask.

"Do you have time to finish up the ironing while I start dinner?" Rosamund asked a few minutes later. "I'd like to get a stew going." She smiled. She knew stew was my favorite dinner, partially because it was one of the few times we had some meat. Stew and spaghetti.

"Sure." At least if I were ironing, I had a good reason for being in the living room when Hans came in, between patients. Otherwise, someone was sure to ask if I'd done my homework yet. Maybe Rosamund was having stew to make me feel better because I couldn't go. No, she must have bought the beef in the morning. I'd never known anyone so regular in her habits.

I hadn't long to wait. Hans came in humming, rubbing his hands together in the way he had, ready for tea, telling Rosamund about somebody's blood pressure he'd brought down. Not a word about how they were making mine shoot up.

He washed his hands and sat down at the table, leaning over to smell the Talisman roses in a Mexican glass bowl. "Sweeter for being the last," he said, smiling.

Rosamund nodded as she brought his tea and a bowl of raisins and nuts and then sat down across the table, peeling potatoes while she had her tea.

"Found mildew on the roses, though. Won't have many more. Once that stuff starts . . ." Hans's voice trailed off into a sigh.

"Yes, it's a shame," Rosamund said. "There are so few other flowers for the house since the frost." Fresh flowers, beautifully arranged, were Rosamund's reward for housekeeping. She would stand before the kitchen table arranging each flower in its season, and only the rose had a second season, after the chrysanthemums had frozen, and before the first China lilies bloomed.

I slammed the release lever as I attacked the shirt I was ironing. How about me?

Usually I loved to hear them talking during their afternoon tea, warmth and understanding flowed between them—his voice electric, hers a ripple—as they shared their day. And even on this afternoon, when I was mad with impatience, I couldn't help listening, couldn't help rejoicing with Rosamund over the call of a flock of migrating ducks an hour before. Hans had heard them too when he'd stepped out the front door for a moment with the blood pressure lady.

Hadn't the principal even called? Had he simply chosen a more available girl?

Finally Hans turned toward me. He grinned. "Annie?"

I stopped the mangle with a jerk, sending his shirt to the floor.

As I stooped to pick up the shirt, Hans said, "Oh, by the way, Annie, will you be home from that bond-selling spree of yours—Saturday—in time to stay with Roger? Paula has a date, and Mother and I wanted to take in a movie."

"Oh, sure. Sure. Sure. I'll be back. It's just in the daytime . . ." I wadded the shirt up between my hands. He must mean I *could* go. *It was all right.* He only wanted to know if I'd be home in time for Roger. *It was all right.* I sat there, aware of nothing and enjoying everything: the fire, the roses, the smell of freshly ironed clothes, and the stew beginning to smell of bay leaf and garlic. I waited for Hans and Rosamund to ask about how I came to be chosen.

"Oh, thank you!" I said.

"Thank *you*, Annie. Mother and I don't often get a night on the town, do we, Rosamund?" Hans always referred to Rosamund as Mother before any of us, and so I felt like an eavesdropper when he used her given name.

Rosamund laughed. "Every time we plan to go to the movies, you get called on a delivery."

"Don't say that. The Wilkins woman is due next week."

Their conversation ebbed and flowed around me. They'd forgotten that I'd be riding in the tanks. They'd forgotten, *or they didn't care.* After all, how often did someone in this family get chosen to ride around in an Army tank? Never, that's how often.

"Only one girl in each grade gets chosen to go," I said loudly into the first pause.

"So your principal said," Hans remarked and then, after another pause, "he indicated I would be hindering the war effort if you couldn't go, with your father in the service and all."

"Is there much more ironing? We should be cleaning up for supper soon. I could use some help setting the table," Rosamund interrupted with the brisk efficiency she used when she wanted to change the subject.

"I wish I knew what to wear," I persisted, despite the danger signals.

"A gunny sack," Hans suggested.

"Any skirt and a sweater. Surely you don't have to decide now. That's enough ironing now."

"I'm putting it *away*." Couldn't Paula ever help? She was playing scales downstairs, and they grated on my ears. If it had been Paula chosen to ride in a tank, nobody around here would have dropped the subject. We would have heard about nothing else for a week.

All they care about is having me home to babysit Roger, I thought bitterly, forgetting that half an hour before I would have been ecstatic to get permission. All right, I would just go my own way, and when they saw my picture on the front page they'd be sorry, I told myself, forgetting how fat photographs always made me look.

No one said much about my adventure between then and Saturday. Roger did think it might be a tight fit in that tank, reminding me of my claustrophobia (suppose I threw up in a tank?) and triggering nightmares where I got locked in a tank and suffocated because no one heard my cries.

Paula thought they should have let the school elect the girls who rode in the tanks, hinting that the choices would have been much different.

"But they needed someone who could add and subtract to sell the bonds," I replied sweetly.

It was strange, this lack of interest from a family that usually thrilled to anything out of the ordinary. Maybe they just weren't patriotic. Maybe they thought I'd disgrace us all. That was probably it. Then they should be more help in deciding what I should wear. Finally I went to Paula.

"Do you think I should wear the green suit or the tiger-striped dress?"

"Don't wear that tiger dress unless you want to get raped," Paula said.

So, Saturday morning I was wearing the green suit when an army sergeant called for me in a jeep. Two other girls were already in the jeep, girls I knew only by sight. One, Mary Jane Oliver, had been Harvest Queen and her hair had come in curly after she'd had scarlet fever. The other, Carla, was a senior who went with the captain of the football team. They both wore sweaters and skirts.

"Have a great time," Paula said suddenly, hugging me.

"Hey, maybe I can come later and take some pictures," Roger added.

"I'll try to bring you," Rosamund volunteered.

Hans was in the office with a patient and I didn't know whether this was good luck or not. I could tell Paula, Rosamund, and Roger were impressed. Finally! I waved as we drove off and could see them waving back through the windows. I felt tears in my eyes.

What can I say about that day? How can I recapture rumbling through towns and farms in a convoy of Army trucks, waving from the gunnels, leaning on the gun turret, smiling at the tank crew in the brisk cold sunlight of the last day of November, an American flag fluttering from one side of our tank and a California bear flag from the other? The farms themselves, newly plowed for the winter crops, smelled musky and fertile.

It was a sunny, still day, and the crowds were quiet as we screeched to a stop before a post office, soldiers helped us down off those tanks, to the tables where townspeople pushed and shoved for the pleasure of buying U.S. War Bonds. Our bonds. And then they shoved and pushed to take our pictures as we were lifted up to the tanks again. Most people in town had never seen a tank except in the movies. Nor had I.

They cheered as we rumbled down the street toward the next town. And we waved and laughed. I felt as if I were riding a waddling duck, perched on the edge of a gun turret soon to be shipped to the South Pacific, crossed legs dangling against cold metal siding.

I was surrounded by smiling young men smelling

of shaving lotion and hair oil, just out of high school themselves, but muscular, trained in boot camp, looking a generation beyond the boys I knew. Men who could put an arm around me as we rode through town as easily as my dates could put an arm around me in the dark of a movie theater.

I longed for my father and for Hans to see me. However, only Rosamund and Roger and Paula came: Roger to take my picture, and Rosamund to tell me to keep my legs inside that tank before I slipped off. But Paula took pictures too and made her mother follow us through the valley so she could "have a record," and her excitement made up for the lot. She was proud of me, and she said so.

All day we rode and sold, and it was late afternoon before that sergeant and a smiling red-headed private from Virginia brought me home, coming straight through the waiting room and into the living room with me, startling Rosamund into offering them coffee.

They were down on the living room floor showing Roger judo holds when Hans came in from the office.

"I'm learning judo so I can beat the Japs at their own game," Roger said.

"What next, dear God?" asked Hans.

He was soon to learn, for the private and the sergeant wanted to take me dancing, to dinner, out on the town, if not tonight, tomorrow night, or next week, but soon because they'd be shipping out within the month and the good doctor knew what that meant.

He did, indeed. And, even in my delirium, so did I. I prepared to tell my handsome soldiers good-bye when Paula walked in. Couldn't they take us both? I could see they'd be fighting for which one got Paula.

"Those girls are only fourteen and fifteen, and they may not date any soldiers until they are sixteen," Hans said, and his eyes were so fierce neither Paula nor I mentioned that he'd subtracted a year from our ages. The soldiers pleaded their mortality, which was the worst thing they could have done. Hans was terribly nice and gave them each a shot of brandy, but held firm, and after a judo shake with Roger, they reluctantly left. Paula and I were both a little relieved.

"Well, Rosamund, the handwriting's on the wall," Hans said, after they'd left. "Once those hormones get started, it's like lining up bottles. You just can't keep them from flowing into one another. Can't be done," he said gently, lining up a wine bottle and a ketchup bottle on the table, to demonstrate.

"Be pretty hard for those two to equalize," Roger remarked.

Then Hans frowned at Roger, unusual in itself, and when he turned back toward Paula and me, his face was fierce. "There are to be no more servicemen in this house. None. Do you hear me, girls? They are nice boys, probably, *but they are too old for you.* His voice roared through the house, and I found this strangely satisfying.

"Hey, talk to Annie. I didn't bring them," Paula protested.

"But you will. You will," Hans said quietly, his temper gone as quickly as it had come.

Rosamund said nothing but moved quietly through the living room, lighting candles and incense, starting a fire, turning on the lights in the kitchen, setting water to boil. There was something reassuring in watching Rosamund prepare the house for evening, something loving, and I never watched her without pleasure.

But on this evening there was something added, and that was the memory of khaki-covered muscles and the smell of shaving lotion, a strong arm around my shoulder and powerful hands lifting me down from a tank. I had fallen in love with an army, and I wasn't apt to forget the sensation.

11

THE FOLLOWING MORNING I was in the bathroom brushing my teeth when I heard Paula tell her mother that between David and me she felt as if she were dragging a ball and a chain. I turned off the water and settled down on the toilet seat to listen. There was only plasterboard between the bathroom and the kitchen, so eavesdropping was no problem. Nor was I particularly shocked to find myself an eavesdropper. I had learned to lie for Paula in the last few months and found I enjoyed it. Eavesdropping was a natural enough development. Living with my father hadn't given me an opportunity, since he seldom talked with anyone else and, if he did, invited me to join them. But the Raymonds were all secretive and, therefore, vulnerable.

"But I would have thought—you do have a rather different relationship with David than with Anna, don't you? Aren't you lumping them together?" Rosamund's voice held that familiar overtone of amusement. And I didn't blame her. What a crazy thing for Paula to say.

"They both make me feel so—hemmed in. I want to go—whoosh—and get rid of them both."

I could hear her sweeping us both out. Together, I hoped.

"I know it's been hard, Paula. I do know. But isn't Anna making her own friends, beginning to, at least?" I could hear Rosamund setting the table for Sunday breakfast, the only breakfast we all ate together.

"Taking mine is what she's doing. She's so sickeningly agreeable. Last week *my friend* Ruth asked her over for the night."

Rosamund paused. I leaned my ear against the wall.

"And she's so boy crazy. And how come Daddy let her go riding around on those tanks? I'd like to see his face if I came home with such an idea. He'd have a stroke!"

Yes, why had he let me go? I wanted to know that too.

"Well," I could tell by Rosamund's voice that she'd stopped working. If I wanted to talk with Rosamund, I had to peel potatoes or carrots or do something useful that kept me in the kitchen, but, with Paula, she'd stop and they'd sit there talking, doing nothing.

"Well, that was something of a surprise to me, too," she said. The high school principal called up, you know, and Daddy was in the office with a patient. Apparently, he said something about Anna wanting to sell bonds because her father was in the Army, and I gather Anna indicated she was afraid to ask us herself—"

"She would! No guts *at all*."

"Possibly, that's so. Anyway, that made Daddy feel bad and he thought that maybe Anna was lonelier for her father than we realize and the tank tour was only a one day shot and might make her feel closer to her father. Of course, I don't think he expected judo in the living room." I could hear the amusement again, and I smiled, remembering my soldiers.

"Shot out of a cannon, if you ask me. Did you *see* her? And I never hear her talk about her father. You'd think she'd adopted *my* daddy for all she remembers she *has* her own father. *Any* man and she goes out of her mind. You should see her with David!"

"Aaah—"

"Not that I care—particularly—"

The hot water heater came on, drowning out their voices.

"Paula—what's really wrong?" Rosamund was asking when I could hear again.

"Oh—everything. Everything. Never mind. I don't want to talk about it. Well, if you must know, every time Dave and I get together—well, it's just too hard, that's all. Just too much." I could hear Paula's sobs through the wall. Paula wasn't given to crying, and I felt I shouldn't be listening to her. But I didn't leave. I had to know what she was crying about.

"You don't have to go out with him, Paula, just because he wants to."

"Do you think I don't know that? Oh, you'd never understand. Didn't you ever fall in love?"

Well, I hope Rosamund was as startled as I was by that!

"Yes," Rosamund replied. "Yes, I did, Paula."

"Then say something. What did you do? Everytime I'm with him we end up going somewhere and parking. That's what happens."

As if the whole school didn't know that.

"I was older, I guess. We got married . . ." Rosamund said in a remembering voice.

"Mother! Will you please listen to me—just for once. You never listen to me. Please!" Paula's voice was desperate, but I do not know what advice Rosamund would have given for just then the door from the waiting room opened and Hans walked in.

"Paula, keep your voice down. Ready for breakfast, Mother?" he said, probably rubbing his hands together.

So I flushed the toilet and went in with Roger when Hans rang the brass bell that hung outside the back

108

door. There was no trace of Paula's tears, and aside from being sulky with me, you would never have guessed she was in love.

How I envied her. Imagine having a man who cared for you, someone to share everything you thought and dreamed and felt, who would listen and then share his hopes and dreams. And everything either of you did was important to the other. I remembered their gentle love-making of the summer before, and my head swam. I forgot how unhappy love seemed to be making Paula. She and David were the hero and heroine of every novel I read, and I saw myself as the spinster aunt. Always agreeable because otherwise I'd be out on the street. Always wearing a sensible navy blue cardigan sweater.

Then, only a few days later, I overheard the conversation that almost cured me of eavesdropping. I was in the bathroom again. I should explain that I did not have bladder trouble nor did I sit on the john waiting for gossip, but since the kitchen was a half-inch of plasterboard away from the only bathroom, you had to make an effort to avoid hearing. I simply did not make that effort. It was late afternoon this time, and Hans had just come in from the office. I heard my name so I paused and listened.

"That Anna. I thought I was taking on my friend's little girl so he could go off to war, but he's left us a teenager in heat. And with two ports of embarkation in the county, it won't be long before Paula's fuse gets lit.

And they're so innocent. Rosamund, if you saw the girls I see in the office every day—pregnant, suicidal, no older than Annie and Paula; it's enough to break your heart."

I could hear Rosamund asking what had happened, and I was curious too because it seemed to me that my life had been particularly dull since the day I'd ridden on the tank. Even dull enough to please Hans, but apparently not.

And that was it, of course. The tank crew had called and wanted to take me to dinner before they shipped out. Since I knew Hans was strict, I wasn't disappointed that he'd said no. I remembered the redheaded sergeant's strong hands on my rib cage as he lifted me down from the tank. He wanted to see me again.

That mattered. And Hans worrying about me. That mattered too.

Rosamund tried to reason with him, a technique Roger said worked with his father, but only when he thought about the matter the next day. She told him I seemed content, and Paula dated David, who was a nice boy.

I waited for Hans to remind his wife that nice boys made babies, too, but he didn't. Instead he began to talk about the pitfalls of human nature, meaning mine. He was, I gathered, against it. His voice kept rising. If ever a lamb was being hung for a sheep, it was me. I hadn't done a single thing, unfortunately. Paula was the wild one, as she'd been trying to tell her mother.

"Well," Rosamund finally said in what I recognized as her end of patience voice, "if it comes to all that, Anna will simply have to realize that she obeys the rules of this house or she'll have to live somewhere else, just like anyone else."

What did she mean like anyone else? She sure wouldn't send Paula or Roger away if they didn't obey, would she? She would not. But the calm certainty in her voice that she could get rid of *me* if I were inconvenient (which I hadn't been) chilled my heart. *Could* they send me away?

I was just boarding, wasn't I?

Hans switched sides then and told her not to be ridiculous. I was a great kid.

But as I crept out of the bathroom, Rosamund's words settled onto my heart. Perhaps I had always known them, from the moment I had chosen this family over my own, this life over my life with my father. And suddenly the evenings when my father and I sat together on either side of our kitchen table, he reading his newspaper and I reading a book, appeared to me with a terrible poignancy. He would never think of sending me off to live somewhere else because he thought I might go out with a soldier. I was his daughter, just as Paula and Roger were Hans's and Rosamund's children. That was the way it was with parents and children.

The picture of my father and me smiling across the table did not last, of course, was already fading as I left the bathroom, and it occurred to me to blame Paula.

Her recklessness could make them send me away. Who would care if it weren't for her?

12

AFTER A DAY OR TWO the memory of that conversation dimmed a little, and it seemed to me that Hans had said he'd never part with me. I was a great kid, a great kid. He had said that, and I could hear the warmth in his voice.

And when I'd remember Rosamund's voice, I made sure that she would have no reason to send me away. I tried to make myself indispensable around the house. I brought in so much wood that Roger nicknamed me "woodchuck." Crossing the garden I'd see a persimmon fall and remember the persimmons should be picked and mashed and baked into bread for Christmas packages. I volunteered for the applesauce canning. Hans mentioned that his mother had used lavender in her lingerie drawers, and the next afternoon I stripped the lavender bushes and made sachets for all our drawers. Hans and Rosamund could not look out the window at the sidewalks without me rushing for the broom to sweep them. In short, I threw myself into the work of the Raymond household. Fortunately, Christmas preparations absorbed a lot of manic energy.

And crisscrossing the winter garden a dozen times a day gradually calmed me. Every day a different bush or tree turned scarlet or gold. When those leaves fell, I'd notice another and another. And there were winter blooming bushes. One morning the thorny quince bush by my door blazed with pink and white blossoms, like apple blossoms in December. And I'd smell the sweet narcissus popping open even before I'd see them. They seemed to come from nowhere, these bulbs Hans plumped along pathways because his mother always had a pot of bulbs in the house every winter. In Austria.

After school let out, the preparations approached frenzy, heady stuff for a girl to whom Christmas had meant exchanging a gift with my father and dinner at a good hotel. I felt as if I'd stepped inside the *Christmas Carol.*

Paula and I were pooling our money to buy Hans an All-America-winning rose he wanted. We had sent to Los Angeles for the rose and watched the mails daily. Paula fretted because she was afraid I couldn't keep our secret. She said she'd never speak to me again if I told. Roger was also watching the mails, for a sweater he'd ordered for Rosamund.

Rosamund was the clearing house for most secrets as she sat in their bedroom, hour after hour, wrapping presents. Their room was off-limits that week before Christmas, but we could pause in the doorway and talk, staring at the growing mounds of packages lining the walls like a rainbow, corded in silver and gold. And so many! I knew that the Raymonds seldom had cash and though they gave gifts to most of the old and the needy in town, many of the presents had come from the Salvation Army. Rosamund had later made them over. Also, many were practical items for us, saved for the fun of opening them at Christmas. I knew because Roger had sometimes been disappointed on Christmas morning and wanted to spare me that disappointment. I knew because Paula said her father was like a child about Christmas.

Finally, about noon on Christmas Eve, Hans came dragging a Douglas fir up the back sidewalk, so tall that three feet had to be cut from the top, so wide that the organ had to be moved. The tree was nailed to a stand Roger had made in wood shop and stood in the corner, smelling fresh from the forest, waiting.

At lunch we toasted the tree with tiny crystal glasses of mulled wine, glasses only used for such ritual toasts.

Immediately after lunch, everyone decorated. Paula and Roger hunted through to find their favorites, ornaments given Hans and Rosamund when they were babies. My own favorites were a wooden battleship with a string of flags from stem to stern and a golden crescent moon with a disappointed mouth. The lights were bubbling electric candles. There was a Santa Claus as well, the bubbles curling through his beard and giving an aura of laughter to his face, making him look much like Hans.

Hans had been hopping about securing an ornament, mending a light connection, changing colored balls, so the side where Roger worked wouldn't be entirely red—in short, overseeing. But when we unwound last year's tinsel from its cardboard and began to hang it, strand by strand, he sat down at the organ and played carols. And before long, we were singing along with the organ.

Later that evening we were allowed to carry in the presents, which overflowed the tree and were piled high on every shelf and chest and possible resting place. I was particularly curious about three oblong boxes about four inches thick by a foot and a half long and something less than a foot wide. There was one for Paula, one for Roger, and one for myself. Whatever might be in those packages, I was getting the same gift as Paula and Roger. That gift meant more to me than any other.

Then my father phoned from England. I hadn't known it was *possible* to phone across the Atlantic, and yet there was his gentle voice, excited too by talking across an ocean, wishing me a Merry Christmas. He'd gotten my package, and though the persimmon cake was in crumbs, all our English relatives confirmed that they were excellent crumbs indeed. He added that there'd been no bombing yet that day. I tried to tell him about our Christmas tree, but the three minutes were up and there was a click and my father's voice was gone, replaced by a dial tone, as unbelievable as the call itself had been three minutes before.

"I didn't get to wish him a Merry Christmas," I cried, and tears rolled down my cheeks.

Then it was time for another tiny glass of the mulled wine and to bed. And just as I was going, there was another phone call, this one from my uncle and aunt in Washington, D.C., and I wished them a Merry Christmas right off.

Sleep, I thought, was out of the question. I lay in bed listening to the pounding surf, loud on the clear, still night, hearing also the surprisingly dear sound of my father's voice from London. I wondered about those identical oblong presents. And I felt myself drifting off.

The next thing I knew, I heard the sound of the gate bell. It sounded like a cow bell, and I seemed to be surrounded by brown and white cows and their soft underbellies were warm, and there was milk in their udders. But they kept nudging me as I was trying to hurry, and I kept pushing them back, but the harder I pushed the more they turned into clouds, gray, foggy clouds. I was proud of pushing them away with great sweeping gestures, perfect figure-eights, but then I felt as if I were trying to push through water against the current.

It was then I heard the voice. And the voice made me realize my feet were cold. My feet seemed to be bare, and the asphalt I walked on was frozen. At least the cows were gone. But now the voice pushed against me instead, and I found I had to think about what it was saying because it kept on saying the same words over and over again, wanting to know where I thought I was going at midnight. I knew, but I did not know how to put it into words. It was as if the voice was asking me to speak in a language I did not know. But I did know where I was going.

"What the devil are you doing out here in your bare feet at this hour of night?" the man asked.

"I have to go to the post office." It was as light as day, and I looked up and saw a full moon. You could see the new green of the grass and the darker green of the eucalyptus just as clear as if it were morning, under that moon. I had better hurry if I were going to the post office.

"Not in your nightgown, you don't. I'll take you down in the car tomorrow. It'll be closed, though."

"Oh?"

"Say, if you have to go to the bathroom, honey, you're going the wrong way. Better wake up, Annie."

"I'm not asleep." I'd had my eyes open, and I tried to open them again, but it didn't work. I didn't think I had to go to the bathroom, but, now that he'd mentioned it, maybe I did.

"Hans, you know I can't wait until tomorrow. Tomorrow is Christmas, and I have to get your rose bush," I said, and then I did wake up. Suddenly and completely. "Erase that," I said.

"Erase what? Annie, please wake up," Hans said.

"I'm wide awake. What did I just say? Tell me!" I demanded. Paula would kill me if I told about his present.

Then we both turned as the gate bell clanged again.

It was Rosamund, calling. "What is it, Hans, are you all right?"

"Right as rain, Mother. Anna was sleepwalking— on her way to the post office. Would you get her a robe and some slippers, please?"

"For goodness sakes," Rosamund said, and I could hear the gate fall to.

There was that pale full moon, almost white, right over my head, and the sky was a mass of stars, which must be why it was so light. I looked at Hans under the light, and he was right. We *were* standing right in the middle of the alley. Hans put his arm around my shivering shoulders, and that kept me warm down as far as my waist, but I was freezing from there down. No wonder. There were icicles on the tall dry grass that was sticking up a foot above the new green grass.

"Full moon," Hans said.

"I must have been talking in my sleep," I said, excusing myself in case I'd told Paula's secret. If I were sleeping, it wouldn't count, even for Paula, if I told Hans.

"I can't remember what you said, honey," Hans replied. "I'm sorry, kiddo. Rosamund's right. I get you kids too excited with this Christmas stuff."

"Oh, don't worry. I often walk in my sleep on the night before a holiday. My father has hundreds of stories about me. Once I even started hiding Easter eggs in the back yard," I said. We were walking back down the alley toward the back gate now. We had about a block to go, and as we passed yards with dogs, each one would sleepily bark once or twice and give up. I wondered if they had our scent or if they would have done no more about a burglar. I was beginning to enjoy myself, though I was cold. "Please don't tell anyone about this," I said.

"Don't worry, baby. Mum's the word."

But he would. By tomorrow this would make a good story, even better than it was, most likely. And Paula would have a fit.

Rosamund stood by the gate with a robe and slippers, her own quilted satin robe, and it felt warm and silky as I slipped it on. For some reason it reminded me of coming down a red carpeted stairway after the matinee of *Gone With the Wind*.

"Full moon," Rosamund said.

"Sleepwalker's moon," Hans laughed. "This way Anna gets her own private moon."

"I can see where it would be misleading. Moon's bright enough to make you think it's morning already," Rosamund said wearily.

With Hans on one side and Rosamund on the other, I walked back to my cabin and climbed into bed.

13

EVEN WITHOUT the relentless drizzle, it would have been hard to wake up the day after Christmas and realize it was all over for another year, face-to-face with the problems we'd managed to put off and the debts we'd run up. For example, the rose that Paula and I had ordered for Hans had cost almost four dollars extra for mailing and handling, and then it had arrived without a bud or a leaf. Bare root, the catalogue admitted in print only a microscope could catch.

And even our own gifts had been more exciting before they were unwrapped. Those mysterious oblong boxes I'd been so proud about turned out to be nothing more than hot water bottles!

"Mothers," Paula had wailed as we opened these packages simultaneously, choosing them over all the others, and then sat there staring at each other, wondering about those other packages, too. Paula held hers up by her thumb and forefinger, the way you'd pick up a naughty kitten.

"This has got to be the final limit, even for this family," Paula groaned.

Roger and I almost gave up, then and there, but then Paula caught my eye, and I nudged Roger, and he jumped up and started waltzing around the room with his bottle. Hans accompanied him with a Strauss waltz on the organ, and we were laughing so we could hardly get back to opening the rest of the presents.

Those hot water bottles came in handy, too, with the cold rain starting on Christmas day and continuing forever. Every night Paula and I met in the bathroom, filling our rubber bottles, like the Biblical women meeting at the well, Paula said. She named hers *David* even though they had had a fight the day after Christmas.

The rain continued day after day, listlessly and steadily, without the energy of a good driving storm. Withholding weather, Hans called it, so the winter crops stunted, and even the narcissus along our garden walks held their buds and did not open.

Maybe were were all suffering from post partum Christmas, as Rosamund said, but by the middle of January I thought that if something didn't change soon, I'd go out of my mind.

Then things did change, for the worse. One afternoon Paula came home sick. She had a high temperature, chills, and diarrhea. By the end of the week Paula was still sick, and Roger had come down with the same flu. By this time half the town was sick, and Hans was working sixteen hours a day; in the office from eight until six, and then making housecalls until after midnight.

My own flu must have come on slowly, judging from the relief I felt in giving up and going to bed. It was so wonderful to crawl in between ironed sheets and pull a down quilt over me and know I didn't have to move again until I felt better, no matter how long it took. I had a little brass bell etched with monkeys, and I delighted in ringing this bell, in summoning Hans or Rosamund.

And even after our temperatures were down and our coughs were gone, Hans kept us home. His patients were relapsing, often getting pneumonia the second time around. Better to be safe than sorry. He was glad enough to have us stay home and settle into a Monopoly cycle. Paula and David had made up, were as tender with each other as they had been during the summer, and so David arrived every afternoon and we would play until dinner. After dinner we played until bedtime. Day after day we fought over Park Place and Mediterranean Avenue and struggled for monopolies on both railroads and electric companies. Day after day Paula and I competed, ruthlessly foreclosing on David and Roger, and then out-bidding each other for their properties. Every game ended in tears. The loser still would be weeping as he set up the board for another match. Then each night at ten Hans would ring the gong, and we would come into the kitchen for cocoa.

Its preparation was a ritual as serious and ordered as the Japanese tea ceremony it somewhat resembled. Squares of bitter chocolate and honey were melted in a small pan. Goat's milk and butter were added and whisked with a Mexican straw brush to a frothy con-coction before Hans added cinnamon and nutmeg. When the smell of the spices and chocolate filled the kitchen, he added vanilla and the night's special in-gredient. Sometimes there would be a marshmallow or thick whipped cream from the cow across the street, another time a little rum, sherry, or coffee was added. Hans never knew what he would do until the moment arrived. Paula and Roger had their favorites and their barely drinkables, but for me, each variation, each cup of cocoa was a particular treat.

After we'd all been home a couple of weeks, Hans decided the epidemic had run its course enough to send Paula and Roger back to school. I watched Paula and Roger leave for school with a light heart and a slight ringing in my ears.

I remained slightly dizzy and had the curious sense of being off-balance all day. I didn't feel up to Monopoly and was grateful when Paula and Roger had homework. Still, I didn't feel ill, just at a rather pleasant remove from the people and things around me. Then, sometime during the night I woke with a terrible shooting pain in my left ear, a pain I knew because I'd had trouble with that ear before. I stumbled into the house and woke Hans, half-crazy with a pain that burned and hammered into my skull.

He told me to go on into the office and turn on the light and the heat while he pulled himself together.

The office had a calming effect as I sat on the treatment table cupping my ear to ease the pain, listening to the buzz of the heater. It was getting warmer, but I still rubbed my feet together to keep the circulation going, listening now for Hans in the bathroom where he was scrubbing up. All around me were comforting signs of a doctor's order, and the smell of antiflogistine salve, which Hans so often used on our bruised knees. My ear still hurt, but the pain had subsided enough so I could wait patiently in the gathering warmth.

I had never been in the office alone before. I sat on the treatment table and examined Hans's medical degrees, framed in black, hung on the wall across from me, above the scales, next to the enormous bookcases his doctor father had brought with office supplies from Austria. The massive oak desk had come in that shipment from Austria, too.

Hans hurried into the office and turned on the overhead lights which bathed us in a bright white light. He was wrapped in an old blue plaid bathrobe with a cord around the waist, and he smelled of Palmolive soap. He looked cheerful and kept smiling, but seeing him, for the first time, in need of a shave and with rumpled hair, I realized how sick I must be. He laid his short square hand on my shoulder and massaged it sympathetically while the sterilizer heated, and he peered at my ear.

"Poor Annie. Damned ear hurt enough to wake you, did it? Left ear again?" he asked as he picked up a shiny coned instrument that looked like a pastry press. Cold steel brought back the pain, and I cried out as he turned the tip around in my ear.

"Oh, Christ," he muttered a moment later.

I started to cry. He ignored me, still probing the ear.

"Well," he sighed at last, removing the probe and straightening up. "God knows how we're going to manage this one. You've let it get to a pretty mess, this time. Don't you ever learn when these things are coming on? How long has this ear been bothering you?"

He stood over me and his voice seemed harsh, and I trembled, unable to remember the time when that ear had not been in agony. I had had trouble with my left ear before, several times. One time, before we had a car, my father had called a taxi in the middle of the night, and he and the taxi driver had talked about the pain of having their teeth pulled all the way to the doctor. Another time I'd gone by myself in the streetcar downtown to the doctor's office, and I kept getting so dizzy I couldn't see anything but colored balls, and I was terrified that I'd miss my stop and miss my appointment and we'd have to pay for it even if I didn't show up. At the last minute I had seen the stop, but too late to get off, and I'd had to walk back two blocks. I'd been late, but the doctor had seen me anyhow.

"How long?" Hans repeated.

"Oh, sorry. Just since I woke up," I whispered.

He shook his head.

"It's true!" I cried. "I felt dizzy today, but I thought that was just from the flu."

"This is just from the flu, too, you know. Secondary infection. Why do you think I've been keeping you home from school? So you could play Monopoly? I've been afraid this would happen, that's why."

"I didn't do it on purpose, you know," I snapped.

"Oh, I know you didn't, poor kid. I'm just tired. Too much flu, too many secondary infections, and it's gone on too long." He seemed to be talking to himself, his hands folded together as if he were praying, except that

125

he held them against his chin, rubbing his stubbled beard up and down across his forefingers, as if this helped his thinking. He often did this when he had a problem. From time to time he'd peer into the ear again with the pastry-press instrument, and then the pain pounded like a drumbeat. He walked over and turned on another machine and then picked up an instrument, this one with a sharp point, and came back and poked it into my ear.

"Keep still," he growled as I tried to edge away from the probing. Suddenly I couldn't stand it anymore. He felt the earache was my own fault. It would probably be my own fault if I lost my hearing and always had to turn my right side to people for the rest of my life.

"Never mind! Go back to bed and get your precious sleep. I'll take care of myself!" I yelled, jerking my head to get away, inadvertently digging the instrument into my ear, causing such pain that I screamed and passed out, but only for a moment, for I was conscious of what was happening, but through a fog, a gauze, through which the pain became a force apart.

I heard Hans call for Rosamund, heard the urgency in his voice, heard Rosamund reply, and a moment later smelling of lavender cologne, follow her voice into the warm office.

"She got mad at me, tried to get down, and the pain made her pass out, poor kid." Hans said. "She's got a mastoid, and if the infection is this bad already, I think I'm going to have to get the pus out of there or she's going to lose her hearing in that ear."

Of course, he was afraid for me so he got mad. That was his way, I thought, comforted, from behind my curtain of swirling pain. I waited to see what they'd say next, as if I were at a movie theater.

"What should I do?" Rosamund asked, her hand on my shoulder now, patting.

Hans was choosing instruments, his back to us, bent forward over the instrument table. "Just stick around in case she needs you, Rosamund, please. This is going to hurt."

Then the pain hit me again, and I screamed, apologizing; Hans and Rosamund saying scream to high heaven, but hold still, very still, then a searing, terrible pain, and Hans's voice, relieved.

"That's it, baby, you'll feel better soon. The worst is over now, kid. You were a brave girl, a very brave girl. I think that will do it, Rosamund. At least it's all I can do. We'll have to wait and see the next few days. Tomorrow and the next day are crucial."

"Am I going to lose my hearing?" I asked, wondering if I already had.

"I don't think so, baby. But you've got to stay very quiet."

"We can keep her warmer in the house," Rosamund suggested.

Hans must have given me a sedative because I saw luminous, rainbow-colored balls, juggler's balls, carrying the office walls around and around.

All night I drifted in and out of that dream, and it was morning before I realized I was in Paula's room, in Paula's other bed.

I would wake many times in the following days to find Hans or Rosamund by the side of my bed, looking down at me. My recovery was slow and painful, but curiously peaceful. Hans had saved my hearing.

The weather turned warm. I had Rosamund and Hans to myself most of the day and was sorry when Paula and Roger returned, bringing news of school. And homework. They were taking final exams, but I couldn't even think of math and English. I didn't want to think of going back to school at all, let alone choose classes for the next term. I wanted to lie in bed watching the hummingbirds on the fuschias.

However, after a month, I did have to return to school, to long dingy halls filled with other girls' laughter and the shuffling footsteps of boys who were, once again, strangers to me. No one had particularly missed me.

I would have to make up final exams in less than a week. I had been gone so long that I felt as if I were beginning another new school, except that it was worse, for I had to take finals in subjects that were a mystery to me, at the same time I was starting a new semester. What was I doing in this classroom? what was I doing with my life for that matter? and who in the whole school would have cared if I had died? I asked myself as I dragged through the hallways between classes, passing indifferent laughter.

Everywhere, boys and girls were in couples; holding hands as they walked the hallway, kissing on the lawn, going off together in cars, while I stood in line waiting for the bus, in an agony of embarrassment, worse since I was alone. Paula rode home with David these days, having accepted his junior pin and his letterman sweater. They were going steady.

How I longed for a steady boyfriend! I didn't even care whether he wore a letterman's sweater or would listen to my dreams so long as we could walk down those halls together, holding hands. I envied Paula—who claimed she was sorry she'd taken David's sweater—with all my heart. I envied her tears as much as her laughter. She was living.

I had been with the Raymonds almost eight months and still didn't have a boyfriend, not even one to whom I could write the single word love anymore. Even he had stopped answering my letters. What was I going to do? How could I live this way?

14

So THE LIFE OF THE SCHOOL had gone on while I was sick, and I felt like a rock stuck in the middle of a creek when I returned. Eating with Paula's friends no longer satisfied me. I was as lonely and as ashamed as I'd been in eighth grade, even though Rosamund had me looking and smelling just like everyone else. Didn't anything help, then? My father had sent me a wristwatch from England, and I watched it just as I had watched the classroom clock the year before, except that this watch had a second hand and I envied its swift movement. Waiting for the bus, I realized what a relief it had been to run all the way home.

One day when I felt very low, Ruth, one of the group of Paula's friends with whom I still ate lunch, asked if Paula and I would like to go to Sunday night church service with her family. Ruth was a girl who, like me, was something of a dog, a little heavy; she wanted to be a missionary in Brazil. She had been a good friend of Paula's before David came along and took up her time.

"I wish I could, but I have a date," Paula said.

"Sure," I said. "Sounds interesting."

Sunday was the day after a terrible storm. The earth sloshed, birds were silent, the surf pounded ominously, and people talked of little else but washed-out crops and the threat of flood. Tempers were taut. Though my father was not religious and I had never been inside a church, I was glad to have something to do. Neither Rosamund nor Hans had anything against the idea, pleased to see me safely occupied, taking up *something* on my own, even religion.

I wore my first pair of black patent high-heeled shoes, and I finally had a chance to wear the tiger-striped dress I'd bought in San Francisco the summer before. Rosamund lent me a black pillbox hat with a veil that came over my eyes. I could hardly see through the veil, but I didn't mind. Roger said I looked at least eighteen. Ruth had just gotten a driver's license and her father let her drive the car; I was proud to sit next to her.

The only problem was Ruth's parents. Ruth's father and mother were from Stockton, where they'd farmed forty years, and then retired to our town when Ruth was about twelve. Once, when she complained that they were so silent they scared her friends, her mother had said that they'd given up hope of having a youngster long before the good Lord blessed them with her, and she was afraid they'd gotten mighty set in their ways. So set in their ways they had given up talking, apparently.

It wouldn't have mattered except that this was the first time I'd worn my tiger dress, to say nothing of the shoes and veil. What a waste when only such dried-up old figs were going to see me, I thought as we walked up the steps of the white frame church. So I was never so delighted in my life as when Ruth turned and said good-bye to her parents.

We were on our own. I followed her around an outdoor veranda to the Young People's Christian Society meeting, and as we turned the corner, I heard the buzz of male voices. My heart raced.

We entered a large room with a raised stage at one end. The welcome smells of shaving lotion and hair tonic almost overwhelmed me. Groups of soldiers in the khaki of my tank crew lounged around next to Naval air cadets, who were wearing blue serge suits with gold buttons and starched white shirts. There were a few girls, but the ratio was at least a dozen to one.

I took one long look around that first night and knew I'd finally come to the right place. I also knew Hans would say I'd stuck my thumb in the jam pot, and I knew what he'd do—if he found out.

Ruth introduced me around, and every man looked me up and down in my tiger dress, and I could see they meant it when they said they were mighty glad to meet me. After all, I decided, Hans only said I couldn't date soldiers and I'd tell anyone who asked that I couldn't. I sat down and accepted a Coke and a doughnut.

They played a series of games, and they all involved touching. In one game a man chooses a girl and they walk around the block together, sharing their memories of how they found Jesus. I think that was the idea.

A short, blond soldier with hypnotic blue eyes chose me right away. I'd noticed him because of his eyes. They were deep set and round and almost all pupil with turquoise blue irises, and they were fringed in long black lashes. I'd known a girl once with eyes like that, and even in grammar school they'd said she had bedroom eyes. He was deeply tanned and muscular, and when he asked me if I'd do him the honor of walking out with him, he used a soft southern drawl. My legs were shaking so that I could hardly stand up.

We walked hand in hand around that dark block, and by the time we got back Jimmy knew I could not date, and we had decided that the best thing for me to do was to join the choir, which met on Thursday nights. I told him I was sixteen, adding a year. He told me he was nineteen and an orphan from Arkansas. Then he kissed me, and I forgot everything he'd said.

I joined the choir. Hans and Rosamund balked a little at my being out two nights a week, but Paula was out at least that often and her grades were poorer than mine, so they gave in. Considering the options, church was probably as good a place for me as any, Hans said.

However, later that week Rosamund was sitting on the patio drying her beautiful gray hair when I came home from school. Camellias were blooming behind her, and she looked like a refugee from a South Sea island. I told her so.

"You are a romantic, Anna. By the way, you do realize that if you go out to this church business on Sunday and Thursday, you'll have to give up the Saturday night dance?" Rosamund looked up at me, and I realized this was no casual question.

"Oh, sure. No problem," I replied.

"Religion means that much to you? Isn't this rather

sudden?" Rosamund continued, combing out her hair, holding section by section up to the sun to dry.

"I'm not so hot on those dances anymore. And I've always wanted to sing, and they'll teach me. You sing around here all the time, so you should understand that." She sang old hit tunes from her teens, fast-paced jazzy tunes, and they didn't sound like songs a middle-aged mother should be singing. They made me a little uncomfortable. I didn't want to think of Rosamund when she was my age.

"Well, singing is a pleasure, that's true," she said slowly. "But I don't think your father would like you running off to Bible college before he comes home and has some say in your future."

"Don't worry. I've never even been saved. I just want to sing."

"Saved?" Rosamund asked, raising one eyebrow.

"You know. You sit there and the organ plays and the choir sings "*Oh, Lamb of God, I come, I cooooooooome,*" and you're supposed to get up and go down the aisle and kneel and accept Christ. But I just clutch the arms of the pew and wait it out." I watched her closely, afraid I'd said too much.

"Why don't you go ahead and *be* saved?" she asked, surprising me.

I shrugged. "I don't want to. I've never thought about religion, but I don't want to say I've accepted Jesus in his church when I know down deep I don't either accept or reject him."

"Yes, I'd feel that way. Do you think you'll feel less temptation to trot down the aisle if you're in the choir?"

"Yes, because we'll be sitting up behind the minister."

Rosamund concentrated on brushing out her hair for a few minutes. After it dried, she would coil it up in interesting ways. Sometimes, when she'd just washed her hair, she'd stick a flower in the coil, and I hoped she would this afternoon. Maybe a red geranium.

Finally she sighed, so much like Hans that I smiled. "Well, then I suppose you'd better carry on in the choir. You must like the people?" she added.

"Just great, except that Ruth's parents do not say one word after 'good evening' all the way to San Luis, not one word."

She smiled. Ruth's parents were patients, so she knew them.

"What are you thinking?" I asked. She was already coiling her hair, and I began to be afraid she'd go and I wasn't through with our conversation, though I wasn't sure what else I wanted to say. I was tempted to tell her about Jimmy.

"It's probably the drama, the ritual, that appeals to you," she said slowly, "the social life." She seemed to be figuring out herself, rather than having a conversation, so I just picked a red geranium and handed it to her without a word.

"You and Hans could come," the words slipped

out. I held my breath. No, no, no, I thought.

But Rosamund only laughed and stuck the geranium in her hair and said, "Time to get supper started, I guess. It's these first warm days I like, the unexpected ones, don't you? Just stick to the singing, Anna, and better leave the rest alone."

Her advice made sense and I often said it over to myself those first weeks when I was tempted to let my legs carry me down the aisle and be saved or when I had other temptations with Jimmy.

15

AFTER I STARTED going to church, I always seemed to be on the run. I hurried to school and then home to study. I hurried from church to choir practice and from choir out to park with Jimmy and then home so Hans wouldn't know I'd been parking. Always guilty and always excited. Curiously, this was also the first time in my life I can remember feeling *bored*. Couldn't Jimmy ever talk about anything but religion and dying? Couldn't Hans ever talk about anything but his patients and the garden? The least Paula could do was either put up or shut up about David. And Roger was going to turn into a baby bird himself if he didn't think of something else.

Then, toward the end of March, we had an unseasonably hot spell and the Raymond garden burst into bloom overnight. I would stand on the kitchen steps looking down on all that bloom and feel some dark weight lift and leave me deliciously free again. It wasn't only that I'd never seen such bloom before. I don't really know *what* it was, but I would stand in that garden and a kind of peace would pass like a flush over my whole body. I could feel it running in my veins. I could gulp it down in a series of deep breathing sighs and run back into the house and want to hug everyone.

Rosamund said it was only spring fever, and it would pass.

Paula said it was about time I got a little nicer.

Hans smiled and hugged me back.

During this time Rosamund asked Paula and me if we'd like to sleep outside one night while the weather held. Roger and Hans had been sleeping out, and she was curious to see a pair of white owls they'd been talking about. They thought maybe Mr. Steffans's owls had a baby.

They couldn't believe I had never slept in the open before, and I couldn't believe a sky could hold so many stars. And the noise! How did these ancient Indians ever get to sleep with the toads and the crickets and owls? The surf sounded like thunder all by itself.

We lay side by side on five cots near the apricot trees, and blossoms blew down and covered us like snowflakes. Roger was on one side so he could grab binoculars, and Hans on the other so he could run for the phone, since he had two baby deliveries due. One of the girls, Elvira, had been in Paula's class and Hans had delivered *her* sixteen years before, when he and Rosamund had first come to South County.

"But why did you come here, anyhow?" I asked sleepily, lulled by the hot water bottle at my feet.

"Yeah, why *here* of all the godforsaken places?" Paula asked.

"You tell them, Mother." Hans sounded as sleepy as I felt.

"Well, let me see, why did we? For one thing, we were newly married and Hans was just out of medical school and trying to set up a practice, which was practically impossible in those days. Hans had an uncle here and he offered us a one-room house and so we came." Rosamund's voice was gentle, and I knew she enjoyed remembering.

"So we came with the stuff from your grandfather's office in Austria—white elephants but our only belongings—in a cart tied to the car, and a week later Hans's uncle heard of a job in Canada—he was a jeweler by trade—and he packed up and left."

"That was a dirty trick. But you stayed," Paula finished.

"Didn't you have a bed?" Roger asked.

"We sold it and bought another one here."

"At the Goodwill?" Paula asked sleepily.

"Where else?"

"So I hung out my doctor shingle and waited for

patients—and waited—and waited. Fortunately my uncle left us two goats and some chickens and his garden or we'd have starved," Hans took over the story.

"Is that why we're vegetarians?" Roger asked.

"So how *did* you get any patients?"

"Well, Paula, baby, finally after about eight days an old Portuguese farmer brought in his goat. Crazy goat had gone through the canvas roof of a car and broken his leg, and the old man wanted to know if I could fix it, so I figured, why not, and I splinted the goat's leg, and darned if in a couple more days the old man didn't bring in his granddaughter with pneumonia, and pretty soon the whole family was coming in."

"How many?" asked Roger.

"How many Cartagenas would you say there are, Mother?"

"Oh, was it *them*—there must be hundreds." Roger laughed quietly. I knew he was thinking of the time one of the Cartagena boys had flashed his searchlight into our window and startled Rosamund so much she dropped a stack of plates. "They were your first patients?"

I could see Hans nod by the starlight. An owl hooted, and from a eucalyptus tree, then, another owl answered, and we were all quiet, hoping to see the great white owls. The hooting went on another couple of minutes and then stopped. Neither bird left the roost.

"What *I* always wondered is how you met in the first place?" Paula asked, after a while.

"I've told you a hundred times, we met through my high school English teacher, Paula."

"Yes, but that's *all* I know. Don't laugh, Mother."

"Well, she was a patient of Daddy's father, and Daddy asked if she didn't know any nice young girls, and she gave him my phone number, and he arranged to meet me after class one day—"

"In high school?"

"No, I was in college by this time."

"And did you like him right away?" I asked, thinking of Jimmy.

"She must have. They were married in three months," Roger said.

"First, we planned to wait five years," Rosamund continued, laughing softly.

"What happened? How old were you?" Paula asked, and I knew she was thinking about David.

"Go on to sleep. We got married. That's what happened," Hans said. "And then we had you, and then we had Roger, and Mr. Steffans and I built this house and planted the garden, and Annie came to live with us and that is how we come to be sleeping out here breathing apricot blossoms. End of story. Go to sleep!"

"How did you know you were in love, Mother?" Paula's voice was petulant.

"That's a loaded question, Mother. Watch it." Hans chuckled.

"Daddy, please let *her* answer."

"Oh, I don't know if I can. It was all so long ago.

Well, I suppose I'd have to say he swept me off my feet. I'd never met anyone who had so much energy or had such a good time and all those *ideas*, and I realized I liked being with him so much more than what I was doing in college—meeting your father—well . . . it was like suddenly waking up."

We were all quiet a moment, and then Hans and Paula spoke simultaneously.

"Thank you, Mother," Hans said.

"I don't feel that way at all," Paula said. "Sometimes I'm bored with David."

"Me, neither," I said.

"That's because David doesn't *have* any ideas," Roger muttered.

"Take your time, girls," Hans said. "It's a long life."

"Daddy and the party line again. Mother, will I ever feel like you?" Paula asked.

We were all quiet, waiting for Rosamund's answer. I wanted to ask her the same thing.

"I don't know," Rosamund answered slowly. "I don't think anyone can ever know what another person is going to feel—about anything. We're all so different. But I'd rather you concentrated on how *you* feel than on trying to feel the way you think I do. Oh, dear, how did I get into this?"

"You're doing fine," Hans murmured. He sounded as if he was asleep.

Then Paula started to talk about David again, and I lost interest. It seemed to be the same old stuff. But, as I snuggled under the down comforter, I thought that I *was* going to feel the way Rosamund had, whether she liked it or not.

The next thing I knew, it was daylight. The quilt and my pillow and my hair were wet. The fog must have come in sometime during the night. I could hear the foghorn out over the ocean, sounding at thirty-second intervals.

Both Hans and Rosamund were gone, and through the fog I could see lights in the kitchen, so I crawled out of bed and ran for the house. I wanted to know if the babies had been born yet.

16

ONE OF THE BABIES had come. Hans had just returned from delivering a healthy girl to Elvira, the girl he'd delivered sixteen years before, and he was telling Rosamund about it. I could see they were happy about it. Babies brought Hans his greatest satisfaction as a doctor, he always said, even if they did cost him his vacations.

I sat at one end of the breakfast table, still half-asleep, drinking in the warmth of the wood fire along with my cocoa. I tend to hang on to waking because there is a kind of wonder in early morning, and especially on this morning when I had a new baby to think about. I knew Elvira by sight, a shy, awkward girl who'd been in Paula's class the year before. How strange to think of her caring for her own baby. She was only a year older than I was, the same age as Paula. I knew Elvira's mother and grandmother, too, so I could see them celebrating having another girl in the family. Hans said Elvira's ma was only waiting on the delivery to put a pink or blue edge on the baptismal gown she was crocheting.

Later, Paula and I were walking to the corner, half a mile away, where we caught the school bus. The fog was lifting across lupine and poppy fields around us, but we could still hear the off-shore foghorns. And the roosters. I thought of the women and their new baby, who would grow up in this town with a mother and grandmother and great-grandmother, none of which I happened to have. Nor had I ever lived more than two years in one town, unless this war kept me here, which was bad luck to think about. Even so, I knew everyone in town. And if I didn't know someone, I could probably say what family they came from by the shape of their nose or the set of their eyes or the way they walked. Hans had taught me to notice how families looked alike.

The thing was, I knew how wonderful it felt to walk down a street and recognize people, but that new baby and Paula would always take this for granted, would never know that city people were lucky if they knew their next door neighbors. But if I tried to tell Paula this, she'd just say I could have this hick town and she'd take the city any day. She could talk like that because there wasn't any danger of her bouncing along like a loco weed over the towns of the world the way my father and I had. And I knew that I'd do it again, if I could have my father back. Still, I envied Paula and that baby. I wished I belonged here. I still wanted to be a Raymond.

I turned to Paula to tell her about the baby, but I hesitated because she looked pulled into herself this morning. Her long blonde hair, curlier because of the same fog that straightened mine, framed an intent face. She had not spoken since we left for the bus.

"Paula," I whispered. "Paula, did you know your dad delivered a baby girl this morning?"

Her face flushed, and she pushed out her hands, as if to push away my words. "Hah, I'll say I know! All my life, *all* my life, I can't remember a day when Daddy hasn't been waiting for some dumb woman to have her baby, usually someone who can't pay and already has more than she can take care of, and always has each baby in the middle of the night. And half the time he doesn't even get paid, and the next day he's taking it out on me and Mother. You can bet he doesn't yell at those women in delivery. Sweet as pie, the good doctor, for them. I'm the one he yells at when he gets tired. He doesn't yell at you, not even at Roger. This morning, just closing the bathroom door is all I did, but I guess it woke him up and you should have heard the racket—"

"He has to go right out on another case in an hour. She's already in labor—"

144

"Save it. He already told me. Could I help it that the crazy door stuck? I'd just that very minute crawled out of bed, late besides, and here was this crazy man standing there, stark naked, yelling at me like I'd committed murder." There were tears in Paula's eyes. "He doesn't yell at *you*," Paula repeated.

"I'm not a member of the family, that's why," I said.

"I think of you as part of the family," Paula said quietly, and I felt the tears in *my* eyes. She knew. She knew and sometimes it drove her crazy, but sometimes, now, she was wonderful. "Besides," she added, "I'll bet your father doesn't even yell at you. You can talk to *him*."

"If he puts down the newspaper long enough." I laughed.

Then we saw that the bus was pulling up to the corner and we had to run for it, arriving, panting, just as the driver was closing the doors. We both pounded, though we knew he wouldn't leave us. But we'd been close to tears and pounding was a relief.

"You two are the worst in the whole school, do you know that?" the driver asked as we got on.

"Better be damned than mentioned not at all," Paula flipped out and had the bus laughing.

Suddenly, for no reason, I remembered that my uncle used to say that, the one who lived in Washington, D.C., the sculptor. He had another saying, too, about there being two kinds of people in the world, those who saw the new leaves on the trees in the spring and those who didn't.

Then I forgot both my uncle and Paula because Ruth was on the bus, and she reminded me we'd be going out for ice cream after choir practice that night. Which really meant that her parents wouldn't be along so we could take the men back to camp and park for a while. That baby better take its time getting born. Both Rosamund and Hans had been mad last time when I came in late on a school night.

After school I told Rosamund what Ruth had said about stopping for ice cream after practice. We both knew I had no other way home unless she came to get me, and it was twenty miles each way.

"Surely," Rosamund said, "you can find a church closer to home."

She'd looked sad, and the memory of her face hung over me halfway through choir practice.

Jimmy looked sad, too. Gradually I noticed that it wasn't only Jimmy, but all the men looked grim. There was a tension you could cut with a knife. A gloom. We were preparing for Easter, and the Hallelujah chorus usually sent chills down my spine, but this evening everyone kept losing his place and it dragged on like a funeral dirge.

Several soldiers left during the break.

"What's going on?" I asked Jimmy, when we went to the car.

He shrugged, taking my hand and stroking it.

"There's a rumor they may be shipped out, next week or the week after," Ruth said, coming up with her friend, who looked like Victor Mature. There were tears in her eyes.

"But there are always rumors—"

"More than rumors, I'm afraid, little girl." Jimmy's voice was low. "Are you going to write to me?"

I nodded. If this war went on much longer, I'd spend all my waking hours writing letters. I felt numb. Suddenly, I only wanted to get out of there, to leave them all and run and run into the dark night, to keep jogging on until it was dawn or I died, whichever came first. I didn't care. I tried to take my hand away from Jimmy's, but he held on and pulled me so that I faced him, had to look up at him.

"This weekend is my last chance for a leave, Anna. We're restricted to camp after. And I aim to take you out to dinner and dancing before I ship out, you hear?" Jimmy's voice was tight; tender but demanding, almost threatening.

"But you know he won't let me—" I whispered, leaving off as he stared down at me, drowning in the intensity of those blue eyes, unable to look away, unable to meet their demand. I felt faint. Maybe I should tell Jimmy I was only fifteen? Jimmy still gripped my hand and now, with his other hand, he reached over and started stroking my hair.

"Don't you want to go with me, little girl?" he asked.

"He'd never let me," I whispered, remembering Hans's opinion of the tank crew. "But at least Ruth has the car tonight," I added, arching toward him as he stroked my hair.

He smiled then. "I wish we had more time, oh Lord, how I wish we had time," he said.

All four of us were quiet as we set out. Ruth and her date, who was married, sat close together in the front seat, Ruth's full lips quivering, the glasses she wore only when driving blurred with her tears. I didn't see how she could drive with his hands roving the way they did.

Jimmy's arm clutched around me so tight I could hardly breathe, and he kept stroking my head the way he would stroke a cat. I wanted him to kiss me, but he always waited until Ruth stopped the car.

"Baby, what's the trouble?" Ruth's friend finally asked after she'd been crying clear across town. He was from the South, too. I sometimes thought Ruth and I had wandered onto the pages of *Gone With the Wind*.

"I'm afraid. It's not just that you're leaving and I think I'm in love with you, but I'm so afraid," Ruth whispered.

And hearing Ruth's voice, so was I. For the first time in that war, I knew that Jimmy's warm muscular body could be lying dead on a battlefield, stiffening like the young man killed in an auto accident stiffened and turned blue as he lay on the table in Hans's office just last week. And not only Jimmy, but my *father* could be killed and never come back at all. I saw them both, Jimmy and my father, lying face down in mud, twitching like the accident victim had twitched. I wanted to scream, to pound on Jimmy, to throw up. I could scarcely breathe.

"We're all afraid," Ruth's date said quietly, and I thought they were the most courageous words I'd ever heard.

Ruth pulled the car into the park and swung onto a dirt road leading to a little plateau overlooking the town where we liked to park. She drove up onto the rise and shut off the ignition, leaning back against the seat, openly sobbing now. Her date, Ed was his name, took her in his arms.

I looked at Jimmy. He'd said before that he didn't expect to make it back. He had a feeling. Now he looked at me through the darkness and echoed Ed's words.

"Yes, we're all scared damn near to death," he said.

I'd never heard Jimmy swear before. In front, Ruth was on Ed's lap and they were kissing. They made a peculiar smacking sound like the outgoing tide sucking around the railroad pier at the beach. Jimmy hadn't kissed me, seemed to have forgotten me, and I had to listen to Ruth and her date.

"Jimmy?"

Jimmy started then and opened the car door. "Let's take a walk, little girl," he said.

Outside, under the stars, he did kiss me, kissed me until I forgot death. We found a small meadow and sat down, lying back as we kissed, intertwined, our arms around each other, our bodies together.

Soon we were rolling over the grass in each other's arms and Jimmy had his hands inside my pants and that had never happened before and I got scared. I must have jumped, startled by the strength of the feeling he'd aroused in me. I don't know whether I said something or he broke off, but the next thing I knew we were sitting side by side on the grass, both crying, afraid of ourselves, afraid of our future, wracked by feelings so intense I could no more explain them than explain why, given such opportunity, we did not make better use of it. But we only sat there clinging to each other's hands, afraid even to kiss.

"I'm a-coming back for you," Jimmy said, as he pulled me to my feet.

"I can't be responsible if we stay out here any longer, little girl," he said then, and he stood up and we walked back to the car before he kissed me again.

Ruth and Ed shifted slightly in the back seat, and we climbed into the front and sat kissing gently. I tried to tell Jimmy I'd wait for him, words I'd gotten from songs, and he said I was too young to hold to any such promise, but I was to write and he was going to send me a Bible. I wondered what Hans would say about my getting a Bible.

After we dropped the men at the gate before Camp San Luis, Ruth drove home, sobbing hysterically. I kept telling her to cut it out or we'd have an accident, but she paid no attention. Somehow, possibly because it was late and the roads were deserted, we made it home.

The next morning, when I woke up and looked out at the spring garden, the roses in full bloom and the roosters crowing down the alley, the night before felt like a dream and I couldn't believe it had happened. In the morning sunshine I didn't want it to have happened. Particularly, I didn't want to think about the war and death, but I also didn't want to remember us rolling in the grass. I wanted to forget the whole thing. I didn't want to be that girl on the dark hill. I was Hans's little girl, and he'd said I had the hands of a gardener.

So I was not happy to return home from school that afternoon and have Hans tell me that a young man from the choir had called, said he was leaving for the Pacific on Wednesday and wanted to go bowling with me on Sunday night. Hans had decided that I could go, as long as Paula came along. That young man had sounded like he came of a good family and was, at any rate, leaving within the week.

"But, Hans, you've got to be consistent with her. You can't let her go this time and not again," Rosamund said from the table where she sat sorting socks, rolling pairs without holes together into balls, and knotting the pairs that needed mending.

"But, Mother, that young man's going to war, and he only wants to go *bowling*."

"I know, but we both realize that they've been shipping men out almost continually. Anna could be going on a final date every weekend. And Paula won't be far behind, and you know it." Rosamund's voice had an edge of fear. Paula. Paula. Paula.

We were all silent. I was thinking of what Rosamund had said about final dates every weekend, and I felt sick to my stomach. I didn't want another final date, ever, let alone every weekend.

Hans sighed. "I think this has to be the last time, Annie, girl," he said softly.

I nodded. I was condemned to the coming date at the bowling alley, but I was glad that would be the last one. All I wanted to do was to work in the garden and forget.

17

WE GOT OFF TO A BAD START Saturday night. Jimmy was like a stranger, or worse yet, he was like someone I'd known and we'd had trouble. And Paula slapped her date because he tried to kiss her the minute we climbed into Jimmy's borrowed car. She was mad, because she and David had broken up again.

I fully expected Paula to turn right around and demand to be taken home. I hoped she would so I'd have an excuse to go with her. Saying good-bye to someone who might be going off to be killed was not my idea of a date. Rosamund's words—final date—kept rising in my throat like a pulse beat. And I was afraid of finding myself rolling on the grass with Jimmy again, afraid of myself.

However, Paula didn't ask to go home. First she got chatty, then she flirted with the soldier she'd just slapped, and by the time we got to the bowling alley, she positively fluttered. She was worse than either Ruth or me. The men thought she was great.

Then, the minute we walked into the bowling alley, arm in arm with our soldiers, the very first people we ran into were David and his new date. Polly was one of the girls we ate lunch with, supposedly a friend of Paula's. Paula simply waved and kept going, a ploy made easier by the noise of bowling balls smacking pins along nine alleys. I couldn't read much in Paula's face, you never could, but I wouldn't want to be David if he tried to make up after this. I thought he looked sick. He should know; he was the one who nicknamed her Mt. Vesuvius.

I'd never seen such a crowd. Half of Camp San Luis must be spending their last Stateside leave at our bowling alley.

In spite of the crowd, Jimmy got an alley right away, and we settled down to playing. It was too noisy to talk even if we'd wanted to. I began to remember that bowling was one of the few sports I liked. Jimmy apparently did too, and he was good, rolling strike after strike, even attracting his own rooting section.

Paula was good too, much better than I.

"Unlucky in love, lucky at cards," she whispered to me, but her face was flushed and eager. She was playing to beat Jimmy, though I noticed her face also lit up when either her date or I sent a ball down the side. She looked the same way she had when I lost a hotel in Monopoly.

I'd never been good at sports because I was near-sighted and too vain to wear glasses. I'd rather talk. However, on this particular evening I gave the bowling balls my full attention. There is something soothing about sending a ball down an alley and hearing it slam into ten pins.

Between games we talked a little, shouting over the other bowlers. Hans had told Jimmy I was barely fifteen and so he made me promise not to "fib" to anyone else, meaning other servicemen. Finally fifteen was the way I'd thought about my age, but since I never wanted to see another soldier anyway, I promised. We exchanged wallet-sized pictures. He gave me a black leather Bible, which impressed Paula and scared me, and a gold cross to wear around my neck. I tried to think of something to give him—to ward off the evil omens—and all I had was a locket from the boy who taught me to French kiss so I gave him that, for good luck. He was so pleased I felt rotten.

Finally it was over. We were home, and Hans had them in for cocoa. Then they had to stay at camp until they left so nobody would be tempted to desert. Another two weeks and they would be sweltering on some Pacific island the rest of us would only see in newsreels. I didn't know Jimmy, really, but I had come to know how wanting a man felt with him, and I liked him. Perhaps if I had known him a little better, well enough to promise to wait for him, I could have built a gazebo of dreams and it would have helped. Or if my father had been around, he and I could have talked about it. But I had sent my father off to war, too.

I threw the Bible Jimmy had given me into the back corner of my closet and piled dirty clothes, books, games, and shoes over it. The gold cross was more of a problem because it was so pretty. Jimmy had said that my wearing it would keep him safe. I knew it wouldn't and that I could not bear such a reminder on my skin. I considered burying it, but I hated to destroy the delicate cross. If I gave it to Paula, I'd still be reminded. Hans would tease me. I'd never hear the end of it. So I put the cross in my jewelry box, but every time I opened the box there it lay, blazing away.

Finally, one afternoon, when I saw Roger holding his treasures up to the sun, one by one, I ran back to my room for the cross.

"Hey, Roger," I said as offhand as possible, "if I were to give you this cross, could you keep it a secret—not mention it to the family—for a while? It's solid gold," I added and despised the pleading tone in my voice.

Roger looked at me a moment, and then his eyes fixed on the dangling cross. He shrugged and held out his hand. I laid the cross in his callused palm, and it glimmered in the sun, exquisitely beautiful. We both looked at it a long moment.

"Gee, thanks a lot," Roger said, awe in his voice. "I'll take good care of it."

"I know." I also knew he would ask me no questions.

"Thanks a whole lot," he repeated, since I was still standing there staring. I turned, then, and ran back into my room.

The next night I did not go to choir practice, mentioning homework. When I didn't go to church the following Sunday, I told Ruth my family had said I couldn't go until after finals because my grades were slipping. I told the Raymonds church was taking too much time. Rosamund said I was wise to realize it, and Hans grinned and nodded.

I didn't think of Jimmy often. I didn't want to think of him, though I wrote him once a week after writing my father. And I listened for news of the Pacific as well as of England. What having Jimmy go actually did was make me miss my father, though he'd been gone almost a year.

For a while everything that happened reminded me of my father. Remembering what he called "our evening rehash" of the daily news opened some sort of dike in my mind. Paula was right. My father and I *could* talk, and I missed that. What I used to remember as silent evenings had really been filled with snatches of wide-ranging talk; about the nature of the universe, the shape and size and possibility of a God, Kipling *vs.* Shakespeare, who should and who would be the next president, what made the swallows come back to Capistrano. Every wild flower I saw reminded me that he'd taught me their names. Latin as well as common.

Sunday mornings were the worst. Though we had almost never had a social life, there had been a short time when my father's brother and his wife had lived near us, and on a few Sundays we'd had brunch together —lunch for my father and me, and breakfast for them. There hadn't been many of these mornings, but they'd been our only family gatherings, and I'd loved them.

Then, after three or four weeks, this longing for my father subsided, perhaps because I did not mention it to anyone. I've noticed some feelings wither if I don't share them.

Whatever happened, they subsided and I went back to trying to draw closer to the Raymonds. Unfortunately, Paula had also come home for comfort. She was done with David, and if Polly wanted him, good luck to her. And if Paula cried in the night, she said it had nothing to do with *that*. It was in frustration over her trouble with geometry, or so she said. I dreamed of getting her and David back together.

So we were both in retreat and came home. All this was natural enough, a natural disaster as it turned out.

157

The plums were early that year. They were ready to can even before final exams were over.

We all worked on the plums together. No one was ever excused from canning, because the fruit was our basic food for the winter. Of course, Hans did have to see his patients, but he was up hours before the rest of us, sterilizing jars, and he stayed up hours after we were in bed, cleaning the kitchen. He loved to can, and his enthusiasm made those days a pleasure second only to birthday parties for me.

However, this year Paula said she couldn't take final exams *and* help with the canning. Not until geometry was over at least. No one mentioned her breakup with David, but we all knew it had taken a lot out of her.

So Rosamund excused her from helping all during finals week. She told Hans that Roger and I could keep up with her in cutting plums. Hans was furious, but Rosamund held firm and he gave in. He usually did when she insisted and I wished she insisted more often.

I didn't mind because I loved to sit around the kitchen table cutting fruit, loved the squishy juice and the smells of stewing plums and melting eucalyptus honey. Everyone worked together and there was the easy talk of an unhurried but virtuous job. We could choose what records were played and what radio programs we wanted to hear. Neighbors would drop by and stay to help.

And there were always treats. Hans always bought

a Whitman's Sampler and every hour he passed the box and we could choose one chocolate from the diagram on the box top. If you were lucky, you had another chance at the nougat you should have chosen last time.

Best of all, at the end of the day, we could look on dozens of jars of fruit, ready to carry down to the cellar shelves for the winter.

So I didn't mind if Paula worked on geometry. But Hans minded, and Paula minded. She'd keep coming up to the kitchen and hanging around. And she and Hans would snipe at each other. Finally one night she exploded.

"All you do is sit there cutting plums and listening to *Amos and Andy* while my whole life is going down the drain," Paula added. "How am I going to earn a living if I can't get into nursing school?"

"Get married," said Roger.

Stop up the drain, I thought.

"You've been excused to study," Rosamund said wearily from the stove, where she was taking bottles out of the water bath.

"I will never get married in my whole life—if I live to be a hundred."

"What does she want from us, Mother? She doesn't have to do a single thing but study—like a princess— Roger and Annie have to take exams and do the canning too, and they manage. Paula wants us to feel sorry for her too?" Hans's voice had a dangerous edge to it.

159

But Paula paid no attention. She never did. In fact, Paula said, "They're smarter than I am. You said so yourself. So, how can I help that? All I *can* do is work harder." Paula gave me a dirty look, and she turned the same look on Roger, but he didn't look up. Then she and her father stared at each other.

It was Hans who looked away.

I sat there cutting plum off the pits, dropping pits into one bowl and fruit segments into another, juice dripping down both arms to the elbow. My pan of plums was almost full, maybe the last pan, since it must be almost nine. In a few minutes I could give it to Rosamund and she'd dump the plum pieces into jars, which would get a steam bath in the big enamel pan, five quart jars at a time for forty-five minutes. Roger and I had been keeping up. We didn't need Paula, so what was the fuss about?

Paula's eyes narrowed, and she turned on me. "And, as for you, Miss Goody-Two-Shoes, you're so smart, so agreeable. First you take my friends and now you want my family. Go ahead, take them. You get everything you want, anyway. Well, I just want you to know that I *hate* you!"

After taking one look at her contorted face, I believed her. She did hate me. She tried to stare me down as she had her father, but I held. Then she turned and ran outside. I shuddered. I'd never had anyone *hate* me before. So far as I knew, people generally didn't feel all that much about me, one way or the other. It was a long time before I could look up. And when I did, I thought Rosamund avoided my eyes.

None of us said a word after she left. Roger went on cutting plums steadily. Hans looked stricken. He met my eyes, and I saw pity. He'd taken off his glasses, and now he ran his handkerchief round and round the glass while he sighed, over and over.

"Poor kid, poor little lonely girl," he said, and I thought he meant me and got a lump in my throat. Then putting his glasses back on, he stood up and went out the back door after Paula. He'd meant her. He was feeling sorry for *Paula!*

"Just keep cutting, you two. I'll be right back," Rosamund said after he'd gone, and she went off toward their bedroom, pulling the hall door shut behind her.

She still won't look at me, I thought.

"Whew," Roger said, after a while.

"What did *I* do?" I asked. I wanted to ask Roger if his mother avoided my eyes, but I didn't want to risk Roger's honest answer. What I really wanted to do was run after Paula and ask her what she expected me to do, get kicked out because I acted like her? Not everyone could get away with tantrums like yours, you know, I thought. Not everyone can get away with being such a baby. Most people in this world *have* to be agreeable. How come you're so special? How come your father goes running after you. My father wouldn't, not ever. I wouldn't be your sister now if you got down on your knees. I reached for another plum and jabbed it viciously with the knife, thinking she'd have to be sorry if I cut my hand, taking care, however, not to. Paula might say I'd done it on purpose.

"She threw a knife at me once," Roger said. He was still cutting plums with the same slow mulelike rhythm, one plum after another, and he had done a mountain of them. "She'll forget it by tomorrow."

"I won't."

"Don't be silly." Roger shrugged, his tone like his mother's, a command.

"I think these have steamed long enough," Rosamund said cheerfully, coming back into the kitchen. Her face had been freshly powdered, and I was afraid she'd been crying. "I think you've about enough for another batch and that should do it for tonight. Just finish up what's in your bowls," she added, and when she looked at me her glance was pleasant. That was the thing about Rosamund. No matter what happened, she went on doing whatever needed to be done. She took my plums and started scooping them into sterilized jars, pouring honey syrup two-thirds of the way up after she'd filled each jar.

By the time Hans returned, she'd started the last batch, and Roger and I had brushed our teeth and were on our way to bed.

"Paula will be in shortly, Mother," Hans said wearily.

"Go to bed, you two, scoot now," Rosamund said. "Don't be so nosey, Anna," she added, as I hesitated.

So I never knew what they said. In the morning

Paula was polite, and by afternoon she appeared to have forgotten what she'd said. I couldn't forget, but when Hans asked us if we wanted to go to the movies the next night, we all accepted.

If there was a manic edge to my celebrating that night and if I avoided talking directly to Paula, no one appeared to notice. I cannot remember what movie we saw, but I was grateful for the two hours of darkness, two hours where I would not have to make any effort. Why was it that everyone forgot Paula's tantrums but me?

Why didn't I pull her hair out or tell her off, at least? Because I'd never had a fight, that's why, I thought. But I could fight now. I'd faced her last night, and it hadn't been me who looked away. She'd better watch her tongue or she'd find out.

Summer vacation started tomorrow. Paula and I had planned to spend the first part of summer at the beach and then work in the fields the last six weeks. Did she still want this? Did I? Maybe I should go back to church on Sunday nights. It would be something to do. A chance to get away.

18

INTO THIS UNEASY SITUATION Hans's nephew, Louis, came riding the first week of summer, just at sunset, in a white pickup with the first surfboard I'd ever seen strapped to the top of the cab like a barracuda. He looked like Hans, except that his smiling brown eyes were set in a somber face and he walked with a slight limp left over from a club foot, long since corrected except, he said, for a tendency to put his foot in his mouth. He was having back trouble, and his family suggested that Uncle Hans had a way of fixing pesky backs, so he'd hoisted sail and come on down. And, if they wouldn't mind, he'd just spread his sleeping bag in the garden for a couple of weeks and sign on for some treatments. If Hans wouldn't mind, he'd photograph this incomparable garden for an assignment he had, and maybe take a few shots of the nymphets as well.

Louis was in his late twenties and already a well-known photographer. He was one of Hans's success stories, so we all knew who he was. And when Louis added that he expected to spend the next few weeks driving up to Avila beach every day, and he'd take any of us along who didn't mind riding in the back of the pickup, we couldn't believe our luck, even after looking up the word nymphet in the dictionary. He'd also enjoy teaching us to surf, if Hans decided his back could take the spills.

Avila was fifteen miles north of town, set in a clamshell-shaped cove, which was indented enough to miss the fog strip, so you could be lying there, sunburning, while you listened to foghorns blaring up and down the coast. That first morning we drove up and back in fog so thick you couldn't see the white line on the highway; but

then, at Avila, Louis coasted down a steep hill into sunlight; past peeling frame houses, held together by climbing roses and old cars that wedged along their sides. One
paved street with hamburger joints, bars, and bait shops
separated these houses from the beach and a bay as
smooth and blue as any in the Mediterranean. An old
pier ran out from the one intersection, its planks far
enough apart to give me a satisfying twinge of fear in
walking out over the water.

Avila was my favorite place in the world, and every
morning I would clamber out of the truck and lift my
arms to the sun as we hit the sand; a genuine sun wor-
shipper, Louis said. Once the engine was shut off, we
heard only the lapping water and the cries of gulls and
pelicans arguing over clams washed up by the last tide.
Roger said it was like being the only people on earth. In
another hour the beach would be crowded with families
and teenagers and servicemen, but the first hour was
ours, and we made the most of it.

When people did start coming, Roger hiked off to
the tide pools and we wouldn't see him until lunch.
After he'd eaten, he'd leave again and wouldn't return
until time to go home, when he'd come trudging down
the beach with two buckets sloshing water and specimens.

Paula and I checked on Roger occasionally, but we
usually stayed close to Louis, because we were wild
about him and because we were attracting a fair amount
of attention ourselves in our matching red Hawaiian

swimsuits. How curious our buying those twin suits was —one of a series of togetherness gestures—something we would never have done when we were really close. But those suits earned us wolf whistles as we lay on either side of Louis, letting our grudges bake out in the sun.

Then, after two weeks, Rosamund came one day. First she followed Roger to the tide pools and watched him hop from rock to rock as the tide swooshed in, around, and over him. After a while, Roger said why didn't she go on back and read and just admire the specimens he brought and let it go at that before she drowned them both? After thinking it over, Rosamund must have decided he was right.

By the time she got back to us, already shaken, she found Paula and me surrounded by what Louis called the task forces; a fan of young men lying about our blanket, most of them with Army dog tags around their necks.

"My, you girls certainly have a lot of company," Rosamund said, with a significant look at Louis.

"I don't let them out of my sight," Louis replied, crossing his heart. "Don't I warn you men they're off-limits—reserved for the next generation?" Louis asked.

"He offers to teach us surfing *instead*," I remember someone saying.

"We're protecting them, too, ma'am," another man promised.

"Mo-ther, please," Paula groaned.

"It's so lovely here," I said.

"It's the *landscape* you admire, Anna," Rosamund replied drily.

"We were introduced to Anna at church," one soldier offered helpfully.

"Oh, so *that's* it," Rosamund said.

That afternoon Louis gave us our usual swimming and surfing lessons, but he did not pose Paula and me on the beach wall for pictures. And we kept trying to discourage our "task force," but as soon as some left, others took their places. By midafternoon, however, we were alone; Roger was back from the tide pools; and Rosamund, though rather grave, seemed to be enjoying the sun.

At any rate, she didn't stop us from going with Louis, and she said little at the time except that we were to stay together. And keep a better watch over Roger.

A week later the apricots came ripe, and we had not only our crop but a stack of lugs brought by friends and patients who didn't want the doctor's vegetarian family to starve. The bees had a field day on the overripe fruit. It had been a good year for apricots, and all over South County trees sagged under the fruit and had to be propped with two-by-fours. You couldn't walk through town without smelling the tart, sweet fruit with every step you took.

This in itself wasn't unusual in our truck farming valley. You couldn't walk through town without smelling celery in May or peas in June or sweet peas in early August, and the smell of the last fall strawberries almost knocked you over. But there was something special, reassuring and oppressive at the same time, about the smell of a bumper fruit crop. You had to do something about it. You couldn't just let them rot. Or so we thought.

So Louis went to the beach by himself, and we settled down to several days of canning. As canning goes, apricots were a favorite because we liked to eat them and all you had to do was halve a cot and flip out the seed.

The first two days of canning went smoothly enough.

However, by the third day we'd almost caught up with the fruit, so Rosamund let Roger go to the beach with Louis. It would have been a particularly hot day even without steam from canning. Both Paula and I had so many cuts that our whole hands stung with the acid juice. I ached from my waist up. What was left of the apricots were overripe, so we were having to cut them into mushy pieces for compote and jam. The flies were driving us crazy. And then the yellow jackets came through a tear in a window screen behind Paula.

"Oh, no! I won't do it with yellow jackets. That's *too* much. We've got plenty of apricots for winter so why should *we* have to keep cutting just because some idiots who are too lazy to do their own canning dumped fruit on us? No, no, no," cried Paula, swatting at the yellow jackets with her knife.

"Hey, you're chasing them over to me. Cut it out!"
I yelled.

"I'd like to cut out Roger's heart, that's what. How
come he always gets out of everything?"

"Will you two stop it! You certainly don't think I
like standing over this hot stove, do you, day after day
after day? I do it so you'll have something nourishing to
eat this winter. I hate canning!"

There were tears in Rosamund's eyes, and her tears
were rare. I wasn't ordinarily comfortable enough to be
a griper, so it wasn't hard to pull in my horns. Paula,
however, couldn't resist one last comment.

"Well, Roger shouldn't get to go to Avila if we
can't."

I could tell from the look on Rosamund's face that
Paula had made a mistake. However, just at that moment the compote boiled over, and Rosamund had to
rescue what she could of the sticky apricot and honey
dripping down the side of the pot and onto the stove.
When she finally turned back to us, her face had a set
cold look that was worse than anger. I shivered, hot as
it was.

"I know you would rather be at the beach. So would
I. As for Roger, he does more than his share around here,
and you know it, Paula."

Paula shrugged, then as her mother continued looking at her, she nodded and looked down.

"And, furthermore, if you want the sun so much,

I'll give you two hours off and you can sun in the back yard."

Neither of us said a word.

"That's what I thought," Rosamund went on. "It isn't the sun you're missing. Those men at Avila are too old for either of you. You couldn't cope with them. And you can't date them. Why not find boys your own age?"

The words were sensible enough, but I could tell that Rosamund was still mad, so I didn't say what I was thinking, which was that the servicemen were more eager to date us than were the boys at school.

"Look what happened when I went with David," Paula said sullenly.

"What did happen? You never said, you know." Rosamund's voice gentled.

"You want a pregnant daughter? Just keep pushing me on David. It's safer at the beach."

"Ah, poor girl."

Both Paula and I stared. Had *Rosamund* really said those words? And in such a mournful voice? She was stirring the compote, her back to us.

"What did you say, Mother?" Paula asked.

Rosamund turned around then, thinking through what she would say. "Can't you tell that boy to behave, Paula?"

"No," Paula whispered. "Not so it sticks—but at the beach Louis tells them, and we just kid around. It's fun."

"Well, there's that, I suppose. Oh, I'll be so glad

when you girls are grown and on your own." Rosamund pushed her hair back from her face. "So glad."

"Mother! What a horrible thing to say. Don't you love me—us?"

"That's why," Rosamund muttered and turned to me. "Anna, why *did* you go back to that church? Why on earth?" she asked sharply.

I shrugged. I didn't really know. Pride, fighting with Paula, the men, the fact that they were shipping out. I'd begun to associate Aqua Velva shaving lotion with next-of-kin telegrams. Maybe because none of the Raymonds went and I could be myself. If it was a free country, why couldn't I go to church? "Why not?" I asked.

"Does it mean such a lot to you?" Rosamund persisted.

"I like the beach better." The sun and the laughing men out on the sand, where I couldn't get into what Louis called wrestling matches.

Rosamund nodded but said nothing further. She was pouring compote into sterilized jars through a wide funnel and gave this her full attention. I'd begun to get a weird feeling in the pit of my stomach. What was Rosamund driving at? Why didn't she just order me to stop going to church if that was what she wanted?

She went on in this way, wondering what my father would say, telling us Hans worried so about our being with older men—

"But, Mother, some of the girls in my class are married already. We're not children. Daddy delivered a baby for one of the girls in my class, remember?" Paula asked.

"Why not write my dad and see what he says?" I suggested, but it came out sounding like a dare. That wasn't the way I'd meant that—or was it? I was pretty sure he'd back me up.

"But that wouldn't really solve our problem, would it? Suppose your father did say it was OK and we didn't like it, didn't see how we could let it go on, with two children of our own in the house, what then?" Rosamund's voice was gentle.

I began to feel worse and worse. I wanted to say I didn't care about church or the guys or anything but making her feel OK about me, but somehow I couldn't. I'd been used to making my own judgements.

"You don't trust me," I said, low.

"Oh, Lord," Rosamund replied. "If only it were that simple."

"Is Daddy having a fit?"

"But I'm not doing anything at all," I said, feeling trapped. Trapped but not *quite* innocent. I knew all too well what Paula meant about David. How about Jimmy and me?

Paula sat watching us, her eyes narrowed, glad to be out of the hot seat herself, I guessed. There was a slight smile on her lips, as if she were thinking of a man.

As for me, between the heat and Rosamund's third

degree, I felt as if I were in purgatory. If I could get out of that kitchen, even for a few minutes. Maybe I could go to the bathroom. But I sat on. I knew Rosamund had more to say.

"What you girls don't realize is how permanently your lives can change if you get involved with a louse."

"Mother!"

"But I haven't done anything."

"Anna, I *know* you haven't."

"So why don't you trust us?" Paula asked. She loved what she called drawing her mother out.

"We're all human, Paula, and I can't have this house upset *all* the time."

I could end this if I'd only say I'd quit church. That's what she wanted. But I couldn't. I don't know why, but I couldn't.

"Ruth's parents don't mind," I said.

There was a stillness in which I heard buzzing flies and the tick of the cuckoo clock.

"Would you be happier living with Ruth and her family?" Rosamund asked softly. Sadly. "Their ideas do seem more like your own."

"You've always wanted to get rid of me," I whispered, stunned. So it had come. "I'd rather die than live with Ruth's parents." All they *had* was religion and all Ruth had *was* men. But Rosamund could send me there, to keep her family safe. Because I was only boarding here.

"Mother, Anna hasn't done anything *at all*."

"No, no, I won't go." I felt trapped, watching Rosamund.

"Don't be silly, you two. I don't want you to leave, Anna, I only asked if you wanted to." She sighed and put her hand on my shoulder, and I flinched and she took it off. "Well, it will probably all work out."

"Mother, what a terrible thing to say!" Paula did look horrified.

Rosamund nodded. "Whew," she said. "We're all too hot to work. Let's call it quits for the day and start friends tomorrow."

So we were dismissed. Without looking at either of them, I slid out from behind the table and went out the door and to my room, being very careful to walk slowly so they wouldn't think I was running away.

I sat in my room and stared out the window at a bed of zinnias until their reds and yellows and pinks spun in my head and I could finally sob, and pretty soon I knew what it was I'd had with my father all those years of my life. I'd had my own family.

"Daddy, Daddy," I sobbed into the pillow. "Please come home before it's too late."

19

NEITHER ROSAMUND NOR I mentioned that conversation again.

Paula tried, saying first that her mother was always talking "like that" and it didn't mean anything, and then, when I shrugged and turned to walk away, she added "I can't see why you keep going to that dumb church anyhow."

"It's a free country," I said and kept on walking. I didn't know why I did either, except that I was saying I was guilty if I quit now. Let *her* ask me to quit instead of exiling me to Ruth's family and then I'd quit in a moment. But I wasn't about to explain any of this to Paula. After all, if they weren't worried about Paula, none of this would have happened.

"You know," Paula said, walking fast to keep up with me. "You do get it through that thick head of yours that Mother hasn't been sitting around plotting how to farm you out to Ruth's, don't you? Well, don't you? That dubious idea came to her as she was saying it, trying to find some way to keep peace in the house. How would you like to try to be a mother in this house? Anna, look at me!" Paula stood in front of me with her hands on her hips, staring at me.

I stood there a moment, and then I stepped around her, looking down and heading for my room.

"Answer me!" Paula screamed.

I stopped. "All right," I said. "I'll answer you. All you've said is the kind of thing your mother says all the time. Why don't you learn to think for yourself, Paula? And stop patronizing me! Stop it forever!" I'd reached my room and shut the door in Paula's face. I locked it and leaned against it. For once I'd gotten the last word. I'd done it.

She banged on the door a few times, and then I could hear her footsteps retreating down the sidewalk. I'd won. Paula was through. She wouldn't keep begging. That wasn't her style. Still, I leaned on the door, breathing in short gasps. What was so horrible was that Paula thought she could just drag it all out and talk, that getting kicked out was something you *could* talk about. *She* could talk, no one was threatening *her*. No one ever had. No one ever would. She could afford to say anything she wanted, anytime, to anyone. Oh, what was the use of thinking about it. I was too tired to think. Maybe it would all blow over. The Raymonds were always yelling around. Maybe the war would end soon. I looked around and noticed a book by a war correspondent that hadn't interested me enough to finish, and I picked it up and started to read.

The next day we went back to Avila with Louis, and I lay still all day, letting the sun heal me. Paula told me I was making a mountain out of a molehill and I said OK, and after that, we just said what we had to so Louis wouldn't think we were fighting. I wasn't fighting with Paula. She just didn't understand that sometimes there wasn't much point in trying to talk things out. I didn't want to leave. I wouldn't *ever* live with Ruth's family if my life depended on it. My father was in England for the duration, so he wasn't coming back to rescue me.

There wasn't anything I *could* do except lie in the sun and hope something would turn up. And I did feel better by the end of the day.

Louis let me ride home in the cab of the truck with him. Sometimes he rode alone, but usually he would ask one of us, and though he kept this favor pretty even, we were always flattered to be chosen.

"No, thanks," I said at first. I didn't want to have to think up conversation.

Louis merely opened the door on my side and motioned. I climbed in.

We rode for some time in silence. Then Louis began to whistle. He was halfway through his second offering and I was beginning to enjoy it when he stopped and said, "Cat got your tongue?"

"I was listening." There was a pause. "You're a good whistler," I added, uneasily.

"I know. That's why I whistle. Look, when the world's fastest mouth clams up and doesn't say a word all day, she's either got cramps or she's in love or she's got trouble. And I'm as nosey as the next guy. Come on, Anna. What gives?"

"Cramps," I replied and couldn't help grinning.

"OK." A longer pause. "OK, so what do you hear from your dad?"

"He likes being back in London, but he wishes they'd stop dropping bombs."

"Sensible man. What's his outfit?"

"Signal corps." I crossed my arms and looked out the window. Louis took up whistling where he'd left off and finished the act.

"What do you hear from Jimmy?" he asked then.

"He's fine. It's hot, and he reads the Bible a lot."

"You sound fascinated."

I shook my head.

"Well—did you fight with Hans?"

"No."

"Paula?"

"Nope."

"Rosamund?"

"No." I wasn't in the habit of confiding, and so I didn't even consider telling Louis, who could do nothing.

"I won't even ask about Roger."

We both laughed a little, for it would be spectacularly hard to fight with Roger. I wondered if anyone ever had, really.

"You're not pregnant?"

"Oh, Louis, no! Leave me alone. What a nerve. I just don't feel like talking, that's all."

"First time I ever heard that," Louis muttered. We rode in silence for a few more minutes, the engine unusually loud in the void; compelling, so that I found my heart pulsing to its rhythm, and I remembered a picture of an egret breathing fast until he'd fluffed out his feathers for a mating dance. What made Louis want to know if I were pregnant? When Hans hinted I might get into trouble, I was mortally insulted, and yet the way Louis had asked it seemed perfectly natural, like getting a headache. Maybe his girlfriend was pregnant. He'd broken up with his girlfriend before he came. We knew that much because he'd told us. They probably wouldn't break up if she were pregnant.

"OK, little Indian," he said. "I won't bug you."

"Thank you," I whispered, and the gentleness in his voice sloshed around in my head. He kept massaging my arm, and I lay my head on his shoulder, which smelled of coconut oil. So comfortable, so comforting.

And then I burst into tears. All the tears I had not shed in the last two days came pouring out in great gulping sobs. I cried and cried, and Louis smoothed my hair and patted my arm and offered me a handkerchief and held me tighter and made comforting sounds that didn't need to be separated into words or thought about or answered.

And by the time we turned into the gravel alley leading home, to the Raymond's, I felt better. I still didn't feel like telling Louis my troubles, nor did he ask me again.

"Thank you," I whispered.

"Any time," Louis replied, grinning. "I mean that, incidentally," he added, going around to the back of the truck and letting down the tailgate for Paula and Roger to get out.

"Mighty cosy," Paula said, raising an eyebrow.

"So?" Louis replied, his voice cold.

Paula flushed, then shrugged, and walked up the walk to the house. Maybe she'd tell Hans we were necking, and I'd be in more trouble. But I didn't think so because that wasn't Paula's way. She wouldn't do that even if she didn't have a crush on Louis, which she had. Roger was safe. He'd taken one look at my puffy face and given me a warm smile.

I ran to my room and shut the door and lay down on the bed. Outside I could hear the wind chimes as the four o'clock wind filtered into the protected garden. The shrill whistle of the four P.M. freight train, slowing to toss off the mail as it came through town, was no more reliable than that wind. Rosamund's voice came from the kitchen, along with the rattling of pots and pans, but I knew now that rushing in to peel potatoes wouldn't help. I'd been cutting apricots three solid days when she told me to go live with Ruth.

So I lay on my bed listening and remembering Louis's arm around me until Roger banged the gong for dinner. And when I went in, the kitchen was warm and smelled of stew and freshly baked bread. And this dinner was no different from a hundred others. Paula was going out so she wanted me to do the dishes for her; I said I would, and Hans nagged Paula about that. Rosamund changed the subject, getting Roger and even Louis to help her. Louis launched into a funny story about photographing a beer ad, and that reminded Hans of a patient. We all laughed.

Nothing unusual except that I kept feeling as if I

were watching performers in a square dance figure, as we came towards each other, bowed, and moved apart, clapped our hands, and started once again. So why was I so upset? This was simply the way we lived. Nothing would be the end of the world. At the Raymonds there would always be beer barrel polkas in the background.

Then, we heard the horn blast in the back alley, and after Paula left the table, Hans said that boy, David, was just the kind who would leave his engine running on a farm gas allotment, though no one else in South County had a drop of gas for their tanks.

"She's bound to go with someone," Louis said gently and added, "How about a little pinochle?"

"Deal me in, too," Roger said.

"Me too, as soon as the dishes arc done," I added, starting to clear the table as fast as I could so I wouldn't be left out.

Louis sat at the table cutting the cards over and over. Hans sighed, nodded, and shoved in next to him. Louis winked at me to show he'd wait.

Only then did Rosamund speak. "And I can go to bed and read," she said with satisfaction.

"You'd have been a great poker player, Rosamund," Louis said.

"What makes you think I'm not?" she asked, smiling.

"Prove it. We'll switch to poker," Louis replied, but she'd closed the hall door behind her. I could imagine her settling into bed with her book, a small radio turned to country music next to her. Rosamund could look more comfortable in bed with a book than anyone else in the world.

Louis and I were partners, Roger and Hans paired up. One cool, and one hot head Louis said, meaning that he and Roger were cool. I loved playing pinochle, anyhow, but having Louis for a partner while I still felt the imprint of his arm around me certainly added excitement. Every time he winked, I forgot every card in my hand.

Not Roger. He not only remembered every card in his hand but had to figure every card in each of our hands before he could make his play. Even Hans, who was his partner and stood to gain since Roger played to win and usually did, was ready to break his neck.

Of course, Hans couldn't get a single card he needed, hand after hand, and that would make everyone roar.

And that night it was Louis and I, all the way. Every wild chance I took turned up the right card. Every time Louis pursed his lips, Hans thought he had a flush and turned in his cards and Louis would take the trick with a pair of twos. Time after time Roger needed one card for a run or a flush and it didn't come. Hans got good cards, but he lost his nerve and thought ours were better. In the beginning they were. And then it got so we could sense what the other had, Louis and I, a low grade ESP. We were tuned in to each other that night, and Hans and Roger didn't have a chance. I like to think it had something to do with our ride home from Avila. I like to think that just for a few hours we meant a lot to each other, but I don't know.

We were still playing when Paula came in after midnight, and by that time Roger and Hans owed us an arm and a leg in match sticks.

"I could hear you fools laughing all the way down the alley," Paula said as she came in. "What on earth is going on here?" She laughed, too, reluctantly at first, as if it were contagious.

"Just the worst down-home licking I'm taking, that's all." Roger grinned.

"Never saw you grin before when you weren't winning, little brother," Paula said, falling right into the mood. Something good must have happened with her and David, I thought.

"We were *about* to call it quits. *However . . .*" Louis said, cutting the deck in the fancy way he had. "Every man for himself," he said, dealing.

That night we played until the cocks crowed. And, when we were so tired we couldn't think anymore, and happy too, and the first rays of light were coming over the horizon, Louis told us we were good for his soul, maybe we'd even saved his life, but he was well now and he'd better be on his way, trucking along. There was a girl out there in the valley he had to see again now that he had his head screwed on. He'd remember our pinochle game all the rest of his life, he said, bowing himself out the back door into the morning.

He must have already had his things in the truck because it couldn't have been two minutes later when we heard the white truck start, and that was the last we saw of Louis. He'd ridden into our lives with the sunset and ridden out with the sunrise, and that was the way he did things.

20

So LOUIS LEFT, going back to that girl in the picture, leaving the indentation of his sleeping bag on the garden grass and a big manila envelope of photos for each of us, taking his laughter and our trips to Avila along with him. He left before sunrise in the white truck with the surfboard strapped across the top like a barracuda, trailing little cyclones of dust behind him in the alley as my father had when he left a year before.

And this reminded me that I had to do something about my father. Somehow his air-raid-and-Sunday-visits-to-cousins letters had become personal. He asked if I was "all right" and how was it "working out"? He found my letters "apologetic" and a "bit subdued." What had I revealed in those long letters scribbled on a note pad under the Avila sun? My father, of all people, getting personal. His last letter said I'd been hedging and requested answers to a long list of questions.

Did Paula give me a rough time (as he had given his younger brother)?

Did Hans and I get along?

Did I think he was too strict about dating?

Did I have a boyfriend?

Other friends?

How did I like the school?

Did I need money?

Could I talk to Rosamund?

How was I to answer questions like that even if I had known how to confide in him? My father had grown up with his one *younger* brother in a huge house near the Museum of Natural History, where he and my uncle spent every afternoon. They had servants, and their parents, a movie star and a producer, were seldom even in town. So what could he understand of how Hans dominated our household?

Besides that, my father must have his hands full. This was the summer of 1943, the evening news reported small victories snatched from great defeats, and Hitler's armies had goose-stepped across Europe. It looked as if it would be up to the Allied troops in England to stop them. So I began to censor my letters. I pinned the word *sprightly*, a word he'd used to describe my old childish letters, above the desk and set out to make my letters match the word. They came out mostly letters about Roger. I wrote of Roger and his tide pool specimens, Roger and my gold cross, Roger feeding ravens in the pine tree, Roger meditating with Mr. Steffans, and Roger still meditating while he was canning.

But my father wrote that he found me more interesting than Roger. And he asked more questions.

Was I still going to that church?

How about salvation?

How about the choir?

How about boys?

That question about church was a good one. The white frame church was so smothering, so full of the smell of honeysuckle in the hot summer nights that it took an act of will to enter the door. Nevertheless, I still went to church, and I wasn't sure why. There were the men, of course, and the kissing games on those dark walks around the block.

But I had given up the choir, though I loved to sing and the music of that organ swelled in me still. I quit the choir because I was afraid. Every week after choir practice Ruth drove a different soldier up to the deserted meadow where Jimmy and I had rolled in the spring wildflowers. She'd decided to play the field. I was afraid to go with her and with soldiers less gentle than Jimmy and afraid to come home later and face Hans playing his cello, waiting.

So I only went to church on Sunday nights when Ruth's parents sat in the pew in front of us, still and silent as Grant Wood farmers, and Ruth sat next to me and ripped at Kleenex in her lap, that week's tall soldier on her other side. I sat on the hard polished wood, lost in a pleasant melancholy, and I hardly heard the Lamb of God music, no longer worried about salvation. Ruth's parents would drive us gloomily but promptly home. I had almost forgotten my forebodings about soldiers going off to war, but I was careful not to care for one. I'd become a tease, and I felt like a prisoner. And if Rosamund wasn't satisfied, she should be, I thought.

This is how I answered my father in my mind, but when I sat down to write I said that, yes, indeed, Paula and I were working in flower seed fields. Blue delphiniums as far we could see. And I looked out for song sparrows on our way to work because he'd taught me to recognize them. Paula and I picked more comfortably this year, stripping only seed pods already brown and shriveling, no longer tired by midmorning. And, by the way, since he'd asked, yes, of course, I was still going to church. I'd found the choir took up too much time, so I'd quit that. Surely that should satisfy my father since it was about me and answered questions.

And I *was* glad to be back at work. We couldn't go to Avila without Louis, anyhow. He'd gone, and I was free to dream of him under the hot sun and a romance of delphiniums. And I'd felt like an old hand that first day of work as we walked down the alley again, passing Mr. Steffans chanting and splashing his way through his morning washing.

"Poor lonely old man," Paula said a little later, laughing easily, as we passed last summer's haunted Victorian house, its shades still down.

"Want to stop off and visit him?" I teased.

Paula shrugged. "He probably only needs some vitamins," she said.

Then David met us where the highway joined the long dusty driveway, and holding hands, we three ran up the road to meet Big Boy, our old overseer. He was as handsome and leopardlike as ever, and I watched him to see if he held a grudge against me.

"Ah, still the love birds," he said to Paula and David, and then he stood there looking at me, hands hooked into his Levi belt, rocking lightly on his heels. When I was ready to melt into the dust, he smiled and held out his hand. His smile lit up his eyes.

I took his hand gratefully, my heart beating hard.

"Ah, not so big girl even yet," he said softly, still holding my hand, and the men snickered and I could see them sizing me up, and I was oddly pleased and a little shamed. What would he have said if Jimmy and I had done what we wanted, if I were no longer a virgin? Because he'd see it in my face. I was sure of that. That's what he'd been searching out in that long third degree. And I felt he had a sadness for me in what he'd found, and, Lord knows, I was sad enough as I shuffled my feet in the sand.

Ah, what I would have given for a smart comeback! As it was, I could only blush and shrug, and it was Big Boy who dropped my hand and turned away, back to the men, after telling David we could start on the south field. I spent the rest of the morning thinking of what I should have said.

We were picking delphiniums, and beyond our

field lay the fragrant pinks and blues and lavenders of the sweet peas, just coming into bloom. And beyond all the fields lay the purple brown haze of the San Luis Mountains, hedging our valley in soft round hills. Below us spread a patchwork of vegetable fields, threaded by a freeway on which the cars moved like ants, their speed slowed by the distance from which we watched them.

Paula started to whistle, David picked up the tune in his clear baritone, and I sang along, still plotting what I should have said to Big Boy. There was a light breeze.

We sang a lot those mornings, the singing fading into noon pinochle games, a quick swim, and dogged work through the afternoon. Paula and David were tentative with each other, neither friends nor lovers and struggling toward both. Quick to anger, and tender. I felt they were glad I was around. A third person gave them time. And meanwhile we poured our passion into the pinochle games, our legacy from Louis. We were fairly evenly matched, and we staked our pride on those hands.

We were, all three of us, in an interim.

Then one afternoon in August we came home to find a letter for me with Jimmy's APO number. It was curious that the letter hadn't come from Jimmy, but, in a way, I was relieved. Jimmy's letters were hard to answer, to know what might interest him, since he seldom commented on anything I said. We often had unknown soldiers writing to us, and sometimes they were fun to answer. I got a knife to open the letter so I wouldn't lose any of the V-mail message. Then I paused for a moment, always excited about getting a letter that had come all the way from the South Pacific, seeing the sand and the sea and the palm trees. Coming back to the square masculine writing.

It was in pencil. "We've only met a few times," the letter began.

Must be the guy who looked like Victor Mature, Ruth's married date, I thought, and was about to tell Paula when the next words caught my eye.

"So I shouldn't be the one to tell you, but Jimmy asked me to just before he died. He was a brave man. He thought a mighty lot of you, so I said I sure would tell you if I made it out, myself."

I sat there looking at the words. Jimmy had thought he would die, and he had. Out there in the middle of the Pacific on a sandy island under some palm. Just like he'd said. "Even a coconut could fall down and bust a man's head open," he'd written.

The letter went on to say Jimmy had been on guard duty and been killed by a sniper. I tried to see it, him falling, maybe hit from behind, but I'd forgotten his face—except for those solid blue eyes. He'd only been gone three months and I'd forgotten his face. Even though I'd known all along he was going to die, I'd still forgotten his face.

"This man writes that Jimmy is dead," I said aloud, to find out how the words would sound.

"Oh, Lord, how?" Paula asked.

"Oh, no!" cried Rosamund, putting her soapy hands to her face. She'd been washing dishes. I've never seen her do that before, I thought.

"He was shot by a sniper on guard duty. There were some things he wanted me to have and this man's sending them on."

"Oh, yeah? What? If there's some insignia, can I have it? I'm collecting insignia," Roger said.

"I wonder why he wanted you to have them?" Paula asked. She sounded jealous. "Doesn't he have a family?"

I shook my head, no. I thought of the Bible pushed back in my closet. I wished he hadn't thought of sending me even more stuff.

"Oh, Lord, what a day," Hans said, shutting the waiting room door behind him and coming toward us. He looked unusually tired. "That last lady was so fat I had a devil of a time finding her displaced vertebrae to manipulate them." Then he looked at us as he slid into the table nook. "What's happened, Mother?" he asked, already worried.

"Anna just got a letter saying her friend Jimmy was killed in action," Rosamund said quietly.

"Oh, Lord. That nice young man with the China-doll eyes who took the girls bowling?"

I nodded.

"Yes, I'm afraid so." Rosamund set a cup and the steeping teapot before Hans, and he took his hands from his head and placed them around the earthenware pot and I could see that the warmth soothed him.

"This bottomless pit of a war," Hans said. "It takes a fine young man like that and kills him—in the blinking of an eye—and for what? How do they think we're going to replace those young men? You must feel pretty bad, eh, honey?"

I felt the tears in my eyes then, and I knew they were for Hans's sympathy rather than Jimmy's death. What a fraud I was! What was wrong with me? Here Jimmy was sending me some of the last things he had touched in this world, and I was sitting here watching Hans mourn because I couldn't. He was dead. Couldn't I get that through my head? And I remembered his eyes and tried to feel they were watching me, but all I could think was how beautiful they had been.

"Well, it certainly is a shame. Poor boy. But Anna really didn't know him terribly well, you know, Hans." Rosamund spoke gently and slowly, feeling her way and trying to teach Hans and me something at the same time.

I looked up hopefully. It was true that I hadn't known him, must have been, or it wouldn't have been so hard to answer his letters, would it?

Rosamund smiled her little half-smile. "Maybe it

would be a good idea to write that poor young man who wrote you. He's the one who could probably use some cheering up about now."

"Yes, I could do that."

"If he's still alive," Hans said gloomily.

"If he's not, they'll send the letter back," Roger suggested.

"Would you girls like a cup of tea?" Rosamund asked. Tea was a beverage we were only allowed as a special treat.

"Sure!" Paula said. "Hey, can I see the letter?"

I nodded and passed the letter over to Paula. Hans leaned over and read it with her. They both sighed.

"It's kind of creepy, don't you think?" Paula asked. "I've never known anyone who was killed before."

"I don't think I have, either," I said, wondering.

"How about old man Bernudi?" Roger asked.

"He must have been a hundred. Jimmy was only three years older than I am," said Paula.

"He died though, and we knew him," Roger insisted. "He had already been reincarnated, too. He'd been a monk in Italy before, in the Middle Ages, Mr. Bernudi."

"So Mr. Steffans said."

"But suppose Mr. Bernudi did have another, earlier life, Paula, and maybe Jimmy is going to have another one." Roger persisted.

Maybe—but I didn't want to think about Jimmy as

a new baby again, and I got up and slid out from behind the table. Everyone stopped talking, and I could see they were watching me. Waiting.

"I just want to go outside for a while," I said.

"OK, honey. I know it's rough," Hans said.

"Hans, let that girl make up her own mind about her feelings," I heard Rosamund say after I had left the room. I was surprised how stern her voice sounded. It comforted me.

I walked through the garden over to a corner beyond the guest house where I knew no one was apt to come. It was a favorite place for me because I could see the orchard, the roses, and the flower beds leading to the house. I put my arms around the trunk of a lemon tree and tried to forget everything but the smell of lemons and the sun warming my back.

But the garden was disappointing. It looked tired. This was the last of August, after all. The zinnia plants were rangy, and mildew wrinkled their leaves. The roses still bloomed, but there were few buds and the leaves were yellow. Over in the orchard, where the fruit had been harvested, the trees looked used up, waiting for their leaves to drop so they could go dormant and begin a new cycle. Even the aged persimmon, whose leaves would turn scarlet after the first frost and then fall in one wind, leaving beautiful orange fruit on bare limbs, even the persimmon tree looked stagnant this afternoon.

And I felt exactly the way the garden looked. Used up. I would have liked to go to bed and read, not for an afternoon but for twenty years. What was the use of struggling? If my father were here, that was the sort of question I could have asked him. It wouldn't have frightened him as it did most people. Me, for example. It frightened me.

Well, at least I wasn't going to pretend about Jimmy. Rosamund had said I didn't know him very well, and she was right. We went to church and did some necking, and then we had that one night when we could have made love and we didn't. And he died at nineteen, only four years older than I was. He'd lived only four more years than I and there he was lying out on that beach stiff and tanned, with the water lapping about him. Nineteen. And suddenly I *could* see his face, the solid jaw and cheekbones and the overhanging forehead and the sensuous full mouth that I'd traced with my finger. He wasn't all blue eyes anymore. He was a beautiful man.

I heard a grunt. Over in the next yard Mr. Steffans was hoeing his tomatoes, deepening the irrigation bowls around them. He worked slowly, grunting, probably without knowing he was groaning. He was so used to the pain. His arms and legs were more swollen than they'd been a few months before. He was getting worse. Hans said he knew he'd never get better, that it would be downhill all the way for him. And he'd certainly known lots of other people who died. His own relatives on Crete, for example. And Rosamund always said the only places Mr. Steffans was sure to go were to weddings or funerals. So he could take it in his stride. He didn't get hysterical. I could probably talk to him. He'd understand.

But I didn't. I stayed where I was, leaning on the lemon tree, but I watched Mr. Steffans, and just watching him made me feel better. That was the way it had been with my father, too.

I don't know how long I stayed there. Until I got goose pimples. No one came out of the house. I began to wish Hans would come out to water so I could ask him if it hurt a lot, getting shot like Jimmy had. He saw shooting victims on Saturday nights fairly often, and recently one man had died right on the treatment table. So Hans would know.

I could hear them talking and rattling pans in the kitchen. Paula laughed, and then Hans laughed. It had a lonely ring in the dusk, their laughter. And I was so cold. I saw the lights on in the kitchen. It must be nearly time for dinner. (It smelled as if Rosamund had a prune cake in the oven.) And still I hesitated, not wanting to bring Jimmy's death, to bring the war into that kitchen.

"Dinner, Anna," Rosamund called.

I got up then, quickly, and ran up the walk and into the kitchen. Released.

That night I had the nightmare—the only one I know, and it comes back when I'm troubled. Each time the dream has something different that I do not remember later. What I do always remember is that I am pursued by a man with a peg leg through endless stone tunnels. They are cool and musty and inside Egyptian pyramids, I think, because there are hieroglyphics on the walls. This man gains only slightly over a long time. As I tire, I can hear him panting also. I do not think he has ever quite caught me, though in my terror I cannot be sure. I woke screaming and found I had torn up my top sheet.

Hey, this is serious, sheets cost money, I thought. I turned on the lights and tried to figure out how I could replace that sheet without anyone finding out and asking questions.

By morning I had decided to buy another one just like it, a flat white sheet, and simply put it on the bed and say nothing. Since I did my own washing that ought to work. Once I had decided this, I felt much better.

Then I realized it was childish to hide Jimmy's Bible, so I took it out of the closet and put it up among my collection of books in the bookcase. The Bible cover was made of leather and the gilt edging was probably gold. I could be proud of that Bible.

Paula told David about Jimmy's death when we got to work, and by noon I had become something of a celebrity. Everyone wanted to see the letter from the man who looked like Victor Mature, and I was sorry I had not brought it along.

21

FOR A WEEK OR SO after the news of Jimmy's death, the only person I felt comfortable around was Rosamund. Hans felt so sorry for me he'd sigh whenever I entered the room. Paula kept giving me queer sideways looks, the way they do in mystery movies. David patted me on the shoulder a dozen times a day. And all Roger could think about was when the insignia would arrive. At the flower seed farm they whispered. Church, once the minister prayed over Jimmy's name on the gold star roll, was impossible. And I'd find myself acting like a heroine in a soap opera, which did nothing for my self-respect. But Rosamund was just Rosamund.

She said it was my turn to learn flower arranging if I'd like, since she'd helped Paula in the spring. So every afternoon after work I'd pick the flowers I wanted and bring them in and choose a vase. Then Rosamund would show me what frog to use, select only a few flowers so each poor flower would have a chance to breathe, and explain proportion. She wanted me to pick in the morning, but the flowers I picked in the morning were never the ones I felt like arranging by the afternoon, so we gave that up.

She had books on flower arranging, but neither of

us liked them. These were my flowers and my design. Rosamund said she felt the same way, she was a make-doer. She also said I had a knack for arranging if only I wouldn't stuff so many flowers in every bowl.

Then one day instead of playing pinochle at noon, Paula and David decided to go for a walk by themselves. They'd been acting more like Ruth and her boyfriends lately, and I was just as glad to be rid of them. In fact, I'd be glad when work was over in another week so I wouldn't have to feel so lonely watching them neck.

So I walked a little in the opposite direction along the creek and headed for a willow clump I knew, to eat lunch. This particular stand of willows must have been used by hobos or large animals because there was a grassy clear spot in the middle like a private room. But when I pulled aside the branches, Paula and David were already there. I let the branches snap back and ran.

I was sobbing wildly and afraid someone might see me so I kept running, all the time afraid of running into someone who would want to know why I was crying.

I didn't know myself. I thought they'd gone in a different direction so I was startled, but watching them neck was nothing new. I didn't want them to think I was spying on them, but that wasn't it, either.

So I kept running and crying and feeling stupid and, inevitably, I stumbled over a root and sprawled on a sunny patch in the path. I lay where I sprawled, gradually letting the sun and the creek soothe me. Far off I could hear the men laughing, so the hands must still be at lunch. I'd dropped my lunch, and I realized I was hungry.

Sitting there in the middle of the path, I also knew why I was crying. I was jealous. Seeing them reminded me that Jimmy was gone and I had no one. I was the only one marching down to the Ark by myself, as my father used to say about himself.

"So, what do I do now?" I asked aloud. But I heard no answer. Everyone seemed to have advice but no answer. Stop being Miss Fantasy Queen of the West was what Paula said. Pick on somebody your own age, Hans said. Don't be in such a hurry to grow up, kid, you won't like it, Louis said. Promise me you won't lie about your age, Jimmy demanded. You'll be a bad influence on Paula, Rosamund said. They all added up to: don't. And I wanted to.

I heard Paula calling and ran to meet her. She looked happy. She should, I thought bitterly.

All afternoon I sang along with Paula and David, listlessly as we did in the afternoon, and later we walked home as usual. But I felt sad and defeated in some way. And the mood hung on. I couldn't shake it. I didn't want to shake it.

I said to myself the thing to do was to get a boyfriend and be done with it. School would be starting soon and I'd have new clothes and Louis had said I was getting prettier every day and so boys would probably be daring each other to brave the waiting room and take me out. But a girl couldn't choose. I couldn't think of a line of boys and take my pick the way a boy could. If I had to wait to be picked by some guy who didn't talk about a thing in the world but his car and how to beat gas rationing, I simply wasn't interested. Though I knew any boy who drove six miles to our house and back had better be interested in gas rationing.

"What ails our Anna?" I heard Hans ask Rosamund. "She's getting as moody as Paula. Can't get a decent sentence out of her. Yes, nope, OK, well—that's the whole of her vocabulary these days, Mother, the absolute whole of it."

"Same thing as Paula. Adolescence," Rosamund replied. I was in the bathroom again, and they were having afternoon tea.

"Paula's better lately," Hans said. "Maybe there's hope yet."

"She and David are back together again." Rosamund did not sound overjoyed. She was no fool.

But Hans wasn't daunted. "Well, honey, there's no accounting for tastes, you know. Look at what you picked."

And, though I couldn't see it, I knew that in the silence they'd reached across the table and taken each other's hands. I waited for Rosamund to say something further about David and Paula, but she didn't.

Instead Hans spoke. "It's not boys with Anna, it's men. Once you get those hormones flowing, they'll find their level no matter what happens, and once she's had the smell of men, those pimply boys at the high school are all going to look like Roger to her. I know. I see it every day."

I felt clammy. And there was a heavy sickness in my stomach. I wanted to beat my head on the wall—or the basin—but I couldn't move, couldn't get that relief. But he was right. Louis, Big Boy, Jimmy. Men interested me. He had my number, all right.

Rosamund laughed. "They'll grow up, and so will Anna, soon enough."

The doorbell rang then, and I flushed the toilet under cover of the second ring. Another patient. Hans would have to gulp his tea. In a moment he'd say, "Well, back to the mines," and wash his hands and go back into the office. And Rosamund would start peeling vegetables for dinner. It was my turn to help. I wanted to help her. The best chance to talk with Rosamund was when I peeled vegetables with her.

But what I did was walk out of the house without saying a word to anyone and down to the beach, and I got home just as everyone else was finishing the dinner dishes. I told myself that Hans had insulted me, though I knew there'd been no insult in his tone. He'd been right, and that was the trouble.

I was grounded for a week.

Three days later we were walking to work, and as we got near the flower fields we heard a great swarm of crows. They sounded like sea gulls, they were so loud. As we came closer, I could see some were circling the fields, and others were cawing from telephone wires and eucalyptus trees.

"What's their problem?" I asked.

Paula laughed then. "Can't you see? Oh, no, you probably can't. I keep forgetting you're blind as a bat without your glasses. Well, they've harvested the sunflowers, and the crows are picketing, that's all. David says they do this every year. Only we quit early last year and missed it all."

Paula quickened her pace, and I had to hurry to keep up. Every morning I watched for the sunflowers, looked forward to watching them turn with the sun as the day wore on and liked to think I tried to keep up with the sun, too. So I wasn't looking forward to seeing them harvested. It wasn't that I cared all that much about crows.

It was those headless stalks standing sentinel around each flower field, still sporting symmetrical leaves like epaulettes, looking like men with their heads cut off. Only a few tagged for special seeds were left, and they looked macabre in the desolation. They reminded me of a print I'd seen once, in black and white, of a line of men where everyone's head was missing except two, who looked bewildered.

"Boy, I'd sure leave them for the crows if I ever had a farm," I yelled at Paula.

"Hey, take it easy. Anna, you're crying. Hey, even Roger doesn't like crows. But if it's any comfort, David feels just like you do. He's going to leave the sun-flower seeds for the crows when he inherits this farm."

I shrugged and sniffed.

"David's a nice guy," I said.

"I know."

"Are you in love with him?" I asked because I'd been waiting for the chance to ask.

"What do you think?" Paula asked gruffly.

"I think so," I said finally, when the stillness and the cawing crows got too much for me.

Paula nodded. Then shrugged and nodded again, giving me a curious smile, half-shy, half-sly.

There were a thousand questions I wanted to ask, and I couldn't open my mouth. All the questions that mattered. Like, how do you know? I wanted to reach out and take her hand. Something.

"Well, at least you're not crying anymore," Paula said finally. "Come on, we're late for work."

I watched Paula turn and walk ahead of me, and something about the way her shoulders slumped seemed terribly vulnerable to me. She had wanted me to go on, to ask her something more about David, and I'd let her down. What was I always afraid of? I watched her a long moment and then ran to catch up.

"Paula, Paula, I'm so glad for you, and jealous too, all at the same time," I said in a rush as I fell into place beside her. I'd forced the words out, the most personal I'd ever spoken to Paula, perhaps to anyone.

They sounded cracked and squeaky, as if I'd hauled them up from the pit of my stomach.

Paula smiled then, a shy, warming smile. She hesitated and I waited nervously, but when she spoke she said only. "I know Anna, thanks. I appreciate that," and quickly asked what clothes I intended to buy before school opened.

And so we talked about clothes, thinking about love, and we were embarrassed, by what we hadn't said as well as what I had. It was hard for Paula to speak her mind, too, I was beginning to realize. Even though she had a family. Still, I'd told her about being jealous, honestly told her, and she didn't hate me. I felt giddy, and as we turned up the driveway toward the marigold fields, I spread out my arms like a bird and ran the rest of the way.

22

"I HATE TO SEE IT END," David said softly the morning of our last day at work. We were sitting on gunny sacks at the foot of our rows, having a cup of coffee before starting. And the smell of the fresh coffee blended with the smell of an acre of marigolds, stirred by the morning breeze. We would be picking velvet giant seeds. David said the fields reminded him of a stadium packed with fans waving orange pompoms as he went over the goal for the winning touchdown. They were too big to be merely flowers, and so we all started thinking of something else they might be, to bring them down to size. It was a clear day and the light cold wind carried a taste of fall, a sense of change rather than of ending, I thought.

"At least this will be your last year of high school, and I wouldn't mind seeing *that* end," Paula said.

"You think I should pick the army or the navy?" David grinned, but I knew he was uneasy.

"Maybe the war will be over," I said.

"Get into college, and maybe they'll defer you."

"Paula, you have to be in some training program. Say, did you know both Big Boy and Charlie Marino are leaving today? Drafted. Army, both of them. I sure don't want to wait to be drafted. Cannon fodder."

"Oh, no," I said.

"Then get in the longest training program you can find," Paula said.

"I'm going to sea. That's it for me. Say, you two want to stay for the cock fight? Big Boy and Charlie are fighting their prize birds one last time before they leave. It's a big deal. Barbecued chicken, wine, beans."

I heard Paula asking if we really could, since cock fighting was illegal and the hands might think we'd squeal. No one had invited us, she pointed out. Then David said he thought it would be all right so long as we didn't tell Hans and Rosamund. He'd vouch for us.

I heard everything they said, but I was thinking about Big Boy going into the Army. Why hadn't he told me? We'd become good friends this year. Wasn't he forever telling me he'd only wait one more year?

"What do you think, Anna? Can we get home in time if we stay? You're the one who's grounded, remember." Paula's voice snapped me back, and I tried to consider. I'd forgotten about being grounded. "Isn't that only for dates?"

"Search me. I've never been grounded. I think so. As long as we get home for dinner."

"Oh, easy. We get off two hours early because it's the final day for summer help. You'll make it," David said.

I'd *always* wanted to see a cock fight. Big Boy and Charlie had the best cocks in South County. Charlie Marino lived down the alley from us and gave Roger feathers, but I knew who I'd be rooting for and it wasn't him.

"Great, if they'll let us stay," I agreed.

All morning the excitement mounted. It ran through the rows, and we kept finding excuses to wander over to the farmhouse and on out under the walnut trees to watch the women and children preparing for the barbecue. They'd been cooking since dawn. Skewered chickens pitched like the ribs of a tepee over one fire, and chili beans and Filipino sweet rice cooked in five gallon drums over two others. Children, babies, and dogs ran everywhere. The air smelled of chicken and chili and saffron and something else, that peculiar gymnasium smell of excitement.

"Which one is Big Boy's wife?" I asked David.

"Can't you tell?" He grinned. "She's the tall dame, the one bossing the others. She's just like him except she talks all the time."

And he was right. I would have known if I hadn't been thinking his wife would be a mouse. She was a big-breasted, small-waisted woman who knew how to move, with flashing eyes and a way of tossing her arms that made her look like she was dancing even when she was stirring beans. Her dark hair hung to her waist, and she'd pinned a pink rose behind one ear. Magdalena. We watched Magdalena ordering the kids in a mixture of Tagalog, Spanish, and English. She was laughing, and the kids laughed, too. I felt lonely and awkward as I looked at Big Boy's wife, his Magdalena.

"Wow, you sure couldn't compete with *her*," Paula said, and something in the wistful way she said it took the sting out of her words.

"Makes me feel like a mouse," I said.

Paula nodded. "Me too."

Reluctantly, we turned and went to pick another row of marigolds. All the hands were in by the time we got back to the office for our checks. The men stood around the farmhouse playing craps and pitching horseshoes, talking softly, and the women were still over by the walnut trees setting food on long tables covered with butcher paper. We lingered with the men since we didn't know many of the women, and Big Boy, who was passing around one of the gallon jugs of Zinfandel wine, offered it to David, daring us.

David took a swig and passed the wine back to Big Boy. Laughing, he handed it to Paula. She hesitated and then took some, though the jug was nearly full and I could tell she had a hard time lifting it to her lips. She handed it to me, lifting one eyebrow just as Big Boy had.

The wine burned my throat going down. I thought I saw a smile play around the corners of Big Boy's mouth as I gulped, and so I grinned and stuck out my tongue at him when I could.

"I hear you're going in the army," I said.

"Drafted. The generals need my help in this war of theirs," he replied, giving me a mock salute as he left.

"I'll root for your chicken," I yelled after him.

He turned and smiled and it lit up his face. He flashed the V for Victory sign. "Good," he said.

David told us there wasn't much worry about the police this afternoon because the two men were being drafted. No one would raid *this* cock fight, unless someone made them.

Pretty soon two trucks pulled up behind the farmhouse, and I could hear cocks crowing inside their canvas-covered backs. I don't know why, but you could always tell the crow of a fighting cock. There was a shrill challenge in the cry, no question about that.

An electricity like a hot wind ran through the crowd when they heard that crowing, and a shiver shot down my spine. Voices rose, and men began counting their money. Once the canvas tops were off the trucks, there was a rush to see the chickens in their cages. And to compare their breeding. Men were shouting—remembering the lines of each cock for brains and power and speed, and for feet. "Show me the breeding, and I'll show you the winner," I heard David say.

Big Boy strode to one of the cages and pulled out a cock, and hiding it with his shirt, he strutted over to the scales, hovering over his chicken, trying to cover it. Teasing. But men pulled his arm to one side, and the crowd gasped as we saw a big blonde bird lift powerful wings and crow, fluttering wings as he crowed, as if he might leave us.

"Too big. No! No! No! Blondie!" The crowd shouted.

"Yippee!" A woman shouted. I couldn't see her, but it might have been his wife from the way the crowd snickered.

"But inexperienced," David whispered.

"How do you know?" Paula asked.

"I know the bird."

Which showed a new side of David, and I wanted to ask him if he went to cock fights regularly, but just at that moment Charlie brought out *his* bird, a glossy red chicken with a luminescent green-black tail, which looked as big and fierce as the white to me. The crowd murmured. He was more experienced, already he'd killed three times and lived.

Money began to change hands.

The crowd sighed when Big Boy and Charlie set their birds down at opposite edges of a ring drawn in the sandy soil. Both men removed the scabbards over two-inch gaff knives attached to the birds' feet and let their birds loose in the dirt ring. Then they crouched on either side of the ring, their faces alert and eager and strangely at peace, the same look on both faces. I kept staring from one to the other, trying to put a name to that expression. Rapt, I decided, just as David grabbed my shoulder.

"Each man will save his chicken, if he can," he said.

I shivered. The knives flashed in the sun. The red chicken looked young, despite its experience, delicate and slender, long through the chest and neck. Big Boy's white bird was stocky, solid, a barnyard bully.

The cocks stood absolutely still for a moment. We held our breath. Then their neck feathers ruffled. They circled the pit.

Suddenly, they hopped right for each other, striking downward, the gaffs on their legs flashing in the sun, the strike raising clouds of dust.

"Ah," the crowd sighed, pushing forward. I can see Big Boy and Charlie crouching, their eyes glued to their birds, but the farmhands have crowded in front of me and I can't see the birds anymore. I push forward.

The only sound is the flapping of wings, terribly

loud, then one bird crows, the other answers, both tentative, and the heavy wings flapping again.

They spring at each other, and though I cannot see, I know by the yell that one has drawn blood, and I push through in time to catch a glimpse of dust caked on bloody gaffs. The birds are two dusty balls of feathers.

Paula is in front with David. I am jealous of her and afraid she'll fall into the ring.

"Paula, Paula," I yell, but she does not hear me.

The crowd yells and then is silent as if half a hundred people are one person. I watch Big Boy. He is possessed. He is beautiful.

"Blanco! Blanco!" the crowd is yelling. What else they yell in Tagalog I do not know.

There is a terrible high squeal. Then silence. Is it over? I peer between legs. Then the sound of the fighting again and murmuring through the crowd. I feel as if I'm going to throw up and I want to get out, but now I am pushed to the front and I see the red chicken bleeding badly before the crowd closes in again.

"Courage, courage," I yell. I want to see. I push and wedge enough to see the red chicken gather itself and go for the kill, tearing into what looks like a ball of dust. They are grunting, like wrestlers, and then I hear the high-pitched squeal again.

It must be over, truly over, this time. Big Boy and Charlie are both in the ring with their birds. Both birds are still alive. How do they know it is over? They know. Big Boy's bird still lives, might even recover they say, but the bleeding red chicken has won a fourth time. He is a real champion, possibly a great champion, and the crowd is satisfied. I look at Big Boy, and I think he is satisfied.

"Daddy is going to kill us," Paula said predictably as she and David stood beside me. She wouldn't let David come with us to explain we had to work late. No, no, no. Paula was worried, distraught. I didn't pay much attention to her.

On the way home we didn't say much. It was twilight, but we would be in time for dinner. We were both crying, but I was crying for some happiness I felt but did not understand, and I believe Paula cried because she worried about getting home late. I didn't want to be bothered by that. I felt I was done with that game.

For the first time since Louis left, I felt light and relieved. The cocoon had burst, and I felt as if I could fly. It was as if I had been carrying around a sack and now I'd set it down and walked away. Why should the cock fight make me feel powerful? It wasn't the fight itself. That made me shudder, though I wished I could keep Big Boy's chicken for him and nurse it back to health. I wished I had said good-bye to Big Boy. I wished he did not have to go into the army.

"We should have stayed for the barbecue," I said, "I feel like I could jump over the moon tonight."

"Oh, Lord," Paula replied, breathing heavily. "That's all we'd need. Can't you walk any faster?" Then, unaccountably, she giggled.

I giggled too, and started to run. As I ran, I smelled the eucalyptus over our heads and the sweet smell of late strawberries in the field beside us and the air in my lungs and the macadam under my feet and the tears, which were still coming, all felt good. I heard Paula calling for me to slow down, but it took a while because I started fluttering my wings as I ran. Finally, when I was able to stop, we were about a block from home, and I was so tired I could have lain down in the road.

"I think I'm going to throw up," Paula said when she caught up. "Cheap wine."

"No, you're not," I said, and she didn't.

We could see Rosamund and Roger in the kitchen because the lights were already on. Roger was setting the table, and he waved a fork as he explained something. Rosamund was standing still, listening.

"He's going to be the handsomest man in the world, Roger is," I said as we walked through the garden to the back door. The garden smelled oppressively of roses.

"Hah!" replied Paula.

"Well, we've been a little worried," Rosamund said as we burst into the warm kitchen. I smelled macaroni and cheese in the oven. "What on earth happened to you two?"

"It isn't dark, yet," Paula said, hastily wiping her face with a scarf.

"Oh, that smells so good," I said.

"But, what's happened? You've been crying, Paula."

"Just hurrying, that's all," Paula said, and I remembered that we couldn't tell. Too bad. I wanted to explain the cock fight to Roger so I could understand it better.

Hans must have seen us because he came trotting in from the garden. His face was flushed.

"Well, what happened to you two?" he asked, putting an arm around each of us. "Mother, get these girls a glass of apple juice."

"Last day of work," I said.

"We had to work a little late, that's all, and we were afraid we'd be late for dinner," Paula said, accepting her apple juice.

"Something else must have happened. You're both crying—or you have been. What was it?" Hans always thundered when he was upset, so his loud voice didn't matter as much as the arm he still had around each of us.

"Never mind. Go wash your hands and faces, girls. Dinner's ready," Rosamund said pleasantly but firmly.

"No! Something has scared these girls half to death, and I want to know what it was," Hans insisted. "See, Mother, they're shaking."

"*You're* making *me* shake," I cried out wishing I'd stayed at the party. Paula gave me a grateful look.

Hans dropped his arms, and we fled into the bathroom. I could hear him telling Rosamund he only wanted to help us, and he didn't know what we'd been up to that brought us home after dark, dirty and crying and stinking of wine, and he wondered who we were trying to protect. I knew Hans was only worried about us, but suddenly I felt terribly weary of his anger. Why did he always have to get angry when he was worried? It didn't make any sense. I didn't want to bother with his anger. It hemmed me in.

All through dinner Hans was sullen and Paula and I were silent. As the excitement drained, I felt exhausted. And I'd forgotten to say good-bye to either Big Boy or Charlie. I wondered if Roger knew Charlie was going to the army, but I didn't ask him. He'd only go down there and load up on feathers.

Rosamund kept darting little worried looks toward Hans. She tried to talk to us about going to San Luis to buy clothes for school. It was only one week until we were to start school. Paula and I both nodded and said, sure, we'd go, but we didn't care.

Finally, as Rosamund dished out blackberries and cream, Hans exploded. "I think I have a right to know where you've been that you come running home like the devil himself is after you. The second time this week Anna has been home late. What do you think this is around here that you come home after dark stinking of wine?"

"We only had one swig. One. For Big Boy, our boss, because he's going into the army. Charlie, down the alley, he's going too. They got drafted is why," Paula poured it all out, omitting only the cock fight.

It was amazing to me that she could say so much and leave out the cock fight.

"I wonder what Charlie is going to do with his fighting cocks?" Roger asked.

"No, you cannot have them," Rosamund said.

"So, it *was* a party," Hans said, but he said it more quietly. He had only wanted to know. I realized we kept secrets from Hans, all of us. "That Anna, she's always kissing some soldier good-bye," he added, trying to make a joke.

But I wasn't in the mood. "I didn't kiss anyone, but I just wish I had! Rosamund, may I please leave the table," I added, icily.

"Just as soon as you tell me why you were crying, young lady," Hans held out a restraining arm.

"Because we were afraid we'd be home for dinner late and you'd have one of your fits and no one could live in this house all night. That's why," I said furiously, pushing against Hans's arm, knowing I was lying. I'd been crying for joy. Because I was happy, something he'd *never* understand, I thought.

He let me out. Then he put his head in both hands. His whole body seemed to sag, maybe he'd had a heart attack, I thought, terrified.

What did I mean talking to *Hans* that way? Everyone at the table stared at me. I wanted to stay and say I was sorry, but sorry was so inadequate, so nothing. The only thing would have been to tell him about the cock fight, *all* about the cock fight, but I *couldn't* do that. Then he looked at me. He was all right.

"Why did you have to make that crack about kissing all the soldiers good-bye? That's what started it all," I whispered.

I left the kitchen without saying another word. Outside, the tinkle of wind chimes in the garden emphasized the silence I'd left.

My father would never have said anything like that because he trusted me, I thought, as I lay on my bed. I was trying not to think of Hans sitting there with his head in his hands. Paula had gone downstairs to practice, and her scales sounded matter of fact and sure. Smug. Roger rattled the dishes in the kitchen, and I thought that the only good thing in the world was that it was his turn to do the dishes.

Sometime later Hans started tuning his cello. Then he played Schubert's *Unfinished Symphony*, which he knew was my favorite piece. The sadness mesmerized me. I could not have moved from my bed for anything in the world. Just as I'd been held earlier by something in the cock fight. I was held again by the melody that floated above the wind and the surf, comforting me and breaking my heart.

The music was his way of saying he wanted me to come back into the house and talk to him and ease our hurt, but I could not.

"It's too late," I said aloud. There was a sudden flurry of crowing from Charlie's fighting cocks down the alley, and I listened until the crowing gradually settled down into complaining clucks, and I knew that, whatever it was, a raccoon or a fox, it hadn't gotten into the pens. The chickens were all right. A fox must have smelled the blood from the wounded chicken.

I'd never talked back to Hans before. I was getting as rude as Paula. I wouldn't think about it. I should get up and take a shower. I closed my eyes again, and a brilliant orange marigold blew apart scattering petals over the darkness. And this time I knew it was the surf I was hearing, a blooming surf. Must be high tide. Tomorrow I would go down to the beach and find some abalone shells for Hans's succulent garden.

23

I KNEW I'D HURT HANS and the hurt kept twisting inside me, too, and neither of us seemed to be able to do anything about it. I hated to look up and see his eyes turn sad as they caught mine, and so, right after dinner, I'd go to my room and hide out. To make matters worse, the weather turned hot and humid and stayed that way until it seemed as if the very sky was pressing down on us.

It couldn't have been more than two or three weeks later that our final blowup came. Paula and I were back in school, but only barely. We hadn't settled all our classes, and Paula was still trying to decide if she needed more math. Everyone in the family hoped she didn't.

Perhaps it was inevitable that my leaving should have come as it did. But our argument was so ordinary, usual even, that I often wonder if I did not set myself up, unable to wait any longer for the break I dreaded, perhaps still hoping that when the smoke cleared I could settle down and be their second daughter.

Whatever. It was a Sunday night and I had gone to church. A still, muggy night such as we often have in our part of California toward the end of September, what Roger calls a night only a mosquito could love. The minister had droned on so that I envied Ruth's father, who was snoring gently in the pew in front of us. There was no air circulating at all in that church, and I noticed Ruth's mother did not nudge her husband as she normally would have but sat fanning herself with a limp handkerchief, perhaps envying him. Ruth tore at her wad of Kleenex, as usual. A tall, dark, muscular soldier with bedroom eyes sat beside her.

Afterwards we went for ice cream and sat on, loath to leave the lazy cooling overhead fans, speculating on whether the heat wave would break without rain. If rain held off another two weeks, both grapes and wheat could be harvested. On the other hand, no one seriously thought we could stand another two weeks of this Canal Zone heat.

Hans was alone, waiting up, when I got home, playing his cello. My stomach sank when I saw him. Lately he'd been playing chess in the evenings with Mr. Steffans, and I'd hoped to see that smiling Buddha face as I came in the kitchen door. But no such luck. Well, I would just say good night. It was too hot to fight. The lights were off, and low candles and incense gave the Raymond living room more the feeling of a church than the stiff, brightly lighted sanctuary I'd left in San Luis.

Hans looked up at me and then back at his watch as I came in. His lips were pursed slightly in a way he had when he was annoyed.

"Have a good time?" he asked.

"So-so. The minister was even more long winded than usual, but Ruth's father took us out for ice cream later and that was nice." I felt edgy, wary.

"That how your lipstick got mussed?"

"Must be." I shrugged. I wanted to go on out to my room, but I knew leaving abruptly was running away, admitting guilt, as far as Hans was concerned. I knew the proper routine, but I was edgy and couldn't resist challenging him, which is what I'd seen Paula do a hundred times and knew led to disaster. I had never challenged Hans until the night of the cock fight, but it seemed to be habit-forming. "Ruth's mother and father were with us every single minute. You can phone them if you don't believe me."

"You're pretty late," Hans said gently and, sighing, began to play again, some mournful piece I didn't recognize.

"How can I help it when they bring me home? Phone

them up. Go ahead. They haven't gone to bed yet." I was pushing hard because I knew Hans wouldn't call, and he knew I knew. But looking at his set, sad face and his hand poised stiffly over the cello, I realized he didn't believe me. I was telling the truth, and the fact that I had lied to him before did nothing to diminish my outrage.

So I stood there and looked at him, and he looked back at me, plucking absently at the strings of the cello. I wanted so much to reach over and make him stop that, but I didn't. I still had that much control.

"The thing is, honey," he said so quietly I had to lean forward to hear, "the thing is that a girl like you has no way of knowing what she's getting into."

"My father always trusted me. You could save yourself a lot of trouble if you did," I said.

"No doubt."

He gave me one furious look and then stroked the cello, hard. But his mad eyes were easier to bear than his sad ones. And it was his fault. I turned to pick up my sweater and leave. I got as far as the door before Hans's voice stopped me.

"The thing is, you're only fifteen. And you're going to end up raped by the side of the road at the rate you're going."

It wasn't that I couldn't hear the anger draining out of his voice, but the words were just too stunning. Or finally stunning enough.

"Well!" I said, whirling back toward him. "How

dare you! What do you think I am, anyhow?" Only bad girls got raped in 1943 as far as I'd heard, and I knew all too well that I wasn't a bad girl.

"Look, Anna, what you are has nothing on God's green earth to do with it. I'm a doctor, and I see these girls, nice girls, younger than you are, crying in my office all the time."

"So, what it really is—you're just worried about Paula," I said, to banish the picture of nice girls crying in his office.

"That too."

I nodded. He'd admitted it. At last. I felt terribly tired. And so hot! It seemed as if we'd been arguing for hours, though we'd said very little. And it all boiled down to Paula. I was a bad influence on poor, dear, little Paula.

"You never *did* trust me from the first day I walked in here."

"Oh, you poor, silly little girl. You don't know what on God's green earth you're talking about. What's trusting you got to do with how you're going to be able to keep some six-foot two-hundred-pound bruiser in line? He could take care of you with one hand tied behind him."

"All you care about is Paula."

He could still deny it if he wanted. But Hans's face was red and angry again, and I was glad that he couldn't pretend to be calm and sensible. A sensible doctor. Paula was wilder than I, and I held this against him, too.

I wasn't tempted to tell him because, even then, I didn't hold Paula to blame for all her parents' attitudes. Still I was glad I had that secret.

"You always wanted to kick me out because of Paula and make me go live with Ruth's parents. But I won't, you hear me, I won't! You can't make me go there."

Hans rubbed both hands across his eyes. "I don't know what you're talking about," he said. Hans's voice was quiet, bewildered, strained. I realized he didn't know Rosamund had suggested I live with Ruth, but I couldn't stop the words now that the unspoken fear had finally burst.

"Tell me, Anna."

"Rosamund said I could go there if I'd feel more comfortable. I'll *go*, all right, but not *there*. I'd die first." Once again the green walls of Ruth's house fused with the windowless kitchen I'd hated in San Francisco, and I was still running. But where *could* I go?

We were silent and so we heard the sliding door to the hall push open, and then Rosamund stood there in her flowered, quilted robe, her eyes still sleepy.

"Why don't you two go to bed," she suggested, and her voice was cold. "It's too hot for this stuff."

"Anna isn't happy with us, Mother," Hans said.

I opened my mouth to protest, but it was true in a way, so I said nothing.

Rosamund merely nodded, her eyes troubled but

steady. She crossed to the rocking chair and sat down and folded her hands in her lap, waiting.

"He—Hans—said I'd end up . . ." I couldn't even say the word rape without crying, and I was not going to cry. Crying was something I'd picked up living at the Raymonds, and I was going to have to cut it out. I certainly wasn't going to break down in front of *them*. "My father," I said into the continuing silence, "my father said I could always go stay with my uncle in Washington if this didn't work out." I whispered the last words.

"Yes, he did say that." Rosamund seemed to be considering. "He told us that, too."

"Is that what you want, baby?" Hans sighed, as he sat looking down at his hands.

"I want to be myself," I said.

Rosamund nodded. Hans shrugged and sighed.

They seemed to be waiting for me to do something, say something more.

"I'll go call my uncle in Washington—right now," I said.

"It's one o'clock in the morning there. Why don't you sleep on it, honey?" Hans suggested. "Why don't we *all* sleep on it?"

Rosamund nodded again.

I hesitated. I looked from one to the other, and Hans kept looking at his hands, and Rosamund looked worn-out, tired of our haggling.

"Go to bed, Anna," she said. "We'll all be more rational in the morning."

"No, I'm going to call my uncle in Washington," I repeated.

We all sat looking at our hands, all three of us waiting for something.

They looked like strangers sitting there with kind, tired faces. Still, I hesitated. Then the mourning of the foghorn broke the moment.

I started for the office. My uncle seemed a logical solution. I even felt eager to see him again, though I had never thought of living with him and his wife before, not even when my father suggested them as a back-up place to live, in case the Raymonds didn't work out.

No one stopped me. I could hear Rosamund's gentle voice, soothing, then Hans's voice, hurt and angry by turns as I sat in the office staring at the scales, the treatment table, the heat lamp, the books—while I waited for the call to come through.

I do not recall how I got the number. My uncle would call on holidays, and he always suggested I call and reverse the charges, but I never had. Never until this one time.

Miraculously, my uncle was still up, and he answered the phone, surprised and delighted to hear my voice, he said. I asked him right away if I could come and live with him.

"Sure," he said, "if that's the way you want to play it."

I remember thinking he could make snap decisions like that and not ask questions because he was a sculptor. Then he did ask if he could speak to Hans or Rosamund, and I called Rosamund to the phone.

They both talked with him, and in ten minutes it was settled. In three days I would be on the train to Washington, D.C. My father had set this all up in case it ever seemed like a good idea, my uncle told Rosamund. His brother was a great believer in contingencies, he said.

I was relieved that it would be all right with my father. I felt I had stood up for myself. I hadn't backed down. And sometimes, it is a relief to lose. You can stop trying and relax. I felt such a relief profoundly that night.

The next morning everyone acted as if there had been no fight.

I had willed myself to forget what Hans and I had said, and I guess he and Rosamund had, too. We were all friendly, and we behaved as though my going to live with my uncle was the most natural and exciting decision in the world. We had agreed to tell Paula and Roger that my uncle had phoned and invited me the night before, and they never questioned us. Paula said I got all the luck in the world. Roger said he'd give me a journal so I could sight migrating birds.

I was so dizzy, so excited, so exhausted, that I was all but convinced myself. We spent the morning making lists. I needed two suitcases, a new haircut, school records, the principal must phone the school in Washington, my clothes must be cleaned and pressed. There were three pages of such items, each to be checked off as it was completed.

There would have been little time to think, even if we moved haphazardly, as casually as my father and I usually did, but Rosamund was an orderly person and she didn't intend to send me off to Washington looking like a waif. There was no telling when I'd get my socks mended again. Roger said it was as if I was moving on a Detroit assembly line, and he was right.

And so two days passed while we concentrated on checking items off our list. Clear warm days, but carrying a salty breeze, the first tang of fall in a beach town. The hot spell had broken the night I'd phoned my uncle. I heard early migrating ducks as I rushed to take my clothes off the line before the evening dampness. I kept moving. We all kept moving, and what had caused all this moving was not mentioned at all.

Paula arranged a party for me at school, and everyone signed the autograph book she'd given me and made me promise to send letters postmarked from the nation's capital.

Only Ruth said, "When did all this come up? You never said a word."

"He just phoned the other night and invited me. He's a sculptor, you know," I said, wondering what I'd say when she asked how come he phoned and invited me out of a clear blue sky.

"You," Ruth sighed, "are about to start living."

I hadn't noticed that my uncle lived more intensely than the Raymonds, but I would be glad to be convinced.

And Paula, how did she feel about my going? She said I seemed to be able to drop in and then drop out whenever the spirit moved me, and she wished she could come to Washington, D.C. I invited her for the following summer, and she said her father would never let her, never intended to let her out of his sight the rest of her life, probably. I could sense the pride under the complaint and it hurt, so I went back to my list.

"You'd miss David too much, anyhow," I said, finally.

"I'll miss you more than I would David," Paula replied quietly.

I stared at her, my heart singing. She'd miss me. And she had come right out and said so. Finally. I wanted to tell her I didn't want to go, that I'd miss her more than anyone, that she was my sister, at least like a sister, a hundred things, but Paula got embarrassed when I tried to tell her things. I said everything awkwardly. And I knew I would start crying. I was on the verge.

So I reached out and caught her hands in mine. She didn't like people to touch her, either, but I couldn't speak. Gently, she pulled her hands away.

"Want me to iron anything' or hem anything for you?" she asked. "You have a lot to do."

"Let me think," I said shakily. We were back on safe ground. I had promised myself not to think about *anything* until I was on that train.

However, on the night before I left, Hans was sitting alone at the kitchen table and he reached out and took my free hand as I passed. The other hand held books to be returned to the library.

I dumped them on the kitchen table and stood there awkwardly, Hans still hanging onto my hand and looking at me as if he'd lost his best friend. It was late; late enough so even the owls no longer hooted in the eucalyptus trees. Everyone else was in bed. I was exhausted and finally terribly lonely, lonelier than I can ever remember being. I still had not written my father about leaving. I had not thought ahead to Washington, had not thought beyond the train.

"Honey, I can't believe you are leaving us. Why do you want to go?" Hans asked. "Here, sit down and have a cup of cocoa with me. He jumped up and poured me a cup before I could gather myself to protest, adding extra cinnamon and then climbing a stepladder to reach the forbidden marshmallows and drop two into the cup. I knew I was leaving when I saw those marshmallows. *Two* marshmallows.

I sat down weakly. Want to go? It was the last thing in the world I *wanted* to do. If I had said anything then, I suppose I would have accused them of not wanting me as they wanted Paula, said that I was leaving because sooner or later they'd ask me to go and I couldn't live under that dread. But I said none of this because I knew I would cry, and I had decided to give up crying. And what was the point?

"We already have the train ticket," was what I finally said, and what Hans accepted. I leaned over to smell an Etoile de Holland rosebud for the last time. Rosamund knew the fragrant deep red rose was my favorite, and I knew she had picked that bud for me.

Hans nodded, carefully placing the cocoa before me, much as Rosamund placed cups of tea and coffee before him every day. He could not have done anything more comforting.

And I am glad I said nothing hateful, for I could not have known the truth then. How could I know that I was half-dead with trying to be a Raymond, that I had to give it up, to go on becoming myself? I knew only that it was over. All over.

Hans and I sat silently for a few minutes, sipping our cocoa. It was a peaceful silence. Our struggles were ending, and we were friends again. I could look at his face, a kind and troubled face, without wondering what he was thinking about me. He looked tired, perpetually tired from seeing too many patients who were too sick by the time they arrived at his office. I could see his affection for me, at least for a moment, without putting it on a scale beside his love for Paula. Or on another scale beside my love for my father. The two of us were simply sitting at the table he'd made to measure for Paula and myself, having a cup of cocoa. I had not cared for cocoa, I remembered suddenly, before coming to live with the Raymonds. Would I still like it in Washington, D.C.? I shook my head. I wasn't ready to think about Washington.

Instead, I looked around the familiar kitchen and into the living room, smelling the incense, watching the ivory candles flicker on each side of the fireplace, fixing every detail securely so I could carry these rooms with me wherever I might go. I was glad there was no music tonight. It was enough to remember how everything looked and smelled. I could add the music later, to suit my mood, as Hans did when he took out his cello.

Then Hans began to talk. Slowly he told me how he had come from Austria when he was fifteen, just my age, and because of my journey he'd been thinking about his. And when he had finished telling me about the birds and the whales and the storm crossing the Atlantic Ocean, he went and got an atlas and pointed out what he had seen coming across the country that I would see in the next couple of days. And we both began to get excited about the Great Salt Lake, and the Rocky Mountains, and the cornfields that fed a nation, and finally, about the capital city itself. I had not given them one thought until Hans showed them to me, gave them to me.

And the Salt Lake and the cornfields and trees turning scarlet along Capitol Hill sustained me through the next morning and through the drive to the train station in San Luis Obispo, when we were all but asphyxiated with the smell of Mr. Steffans's garlic. Mr. Steffans had dressed in a black suit and white shirt for the occasion, a suit neither Paula nor Roger had seen before. Roger wore Jimmy's patch and campaign ribbons, something I'd never seen him do before. I wore the green suit that had given me instant maturity the year before in San Francisco.

It was only after all the excitement of getting my suitcases aboard, making sure I had my ticket and the right seat, kissing everyone good-bye when the whistle had already blown, watching them get off the train and running back to my seat to wave, it was only as I sat in the red plush seat and the train began to move that I knew I was losing them. I could see them huddled together in a knot a little apart from the other spectators —Hans and Rosamund holding hands, Paula waving frantically, and Mr. Steffans and Roger off a little to one side, their heads cocked at the same angle. I'll miss Paula the most, I thought, still measuring. And then, how could I bear it without them? What was I doing here on this train wandering off over the world all by myself when all those I cared about were standing there getting smaller and smaller, staying put, while my father and I were doomed to go where the wars were.

I yanked at the window, pulling it down, and leaned out.

"Paula, Paula, Roger," I called. But the train whistle blew again, and the train picked up speed, and I was beginning to have trouble telling them apart as they huddled together on the platform, growing into one ball as they grew smaller and smaller until I could no longer separate them. I had been leaning out the window waving madly, but now I looked around, embarrassed that people were watching me, and I closed the window. The train curved a little, and they were gone.

I sat back against the red plush seat, numbed, and surrendered myself to the sound of the wheels, the steady rhythm of a train pulling up grade was soothing. I listened and tried to remember what the sound reminded me of, that constant pulsing. And then I knew; within the steady turn of all those wheels, I was hearing the pounding of the surf, coming and going, coming, going. It was almost four o'clock. The winds on the beach must be rising, winds as predictable as sunrise and sunset, Hans used to say.

The door at the end of the car banged open and the conductor started down the aisle. I took out my ticket and held it in my hand as Rosamund had suggested, waiting.